PRAISE FOR WILLIAM SHATNER AND HIS ELECTRIFYING NOVELS . . .

"THE GALAXY'S LOSS IS LITERATURE'S GAIN."
—Kinky Friedman, author of *When the Cat's Away*

TEKWAR
Introducing Jake Cardigan, a tough ex-cop battling a world of high-tech drugs and future shock . . .

"A DELIGHT . . . FAST-PACED, EXCITING."
—Christopher Stasheff, author of the WARLOCK series

"HARD-HITTING."—A.C. Crispin, author of *V* and *StarBridge*

"FAST ACTION!"   —Roland Green, *Booklist*

TEKLORDS
Jake Cardigan fights reprogrammed human "zombies" to pierce the heart of the powerful Tek-Lords . . .

"SHATNER DELIVERS!"   —*Publishers Weekly*

"A COMBINATION OF *MIAMI VICE* AND *BLADERUNNER.*"   —*Locus*

TEKLAB
The ruins of 21st-century London are the battleground for Jake Cardigan and a deadly serial killer . . .

"SHATNER IS A GOOD WRITER and makes good use of concept and plot . . . This reader awaits his next effort."
—*Nashville Banner*

And by William Shatner and Michael Tobias . . .

BELIEVE
The fantastic story of Harry Houdini and Sir Arthur Conan Doyle, two famous men competing in the ultimate contest: to prove—or disprove—life after death . . .

Ace Books by William Shatner

TEKLORDS
TEKWAR
TEKLAB

TEKLAB

WILLIAM SHATNER

ACE BOOKS, NEW YORK

This Ace book contains the complete text of the original edition. It has been completely reset in a typeface designed for easy reading and was printed from new film.

TEKLAB

An Ace Book / published by arrangement with
the author

PRINTING HISTORY
G.P. Putnam's Sons edition published 1991
Ace edition / January 1993

ISBN: 0-441-80011-4

Ace Books are published by The Berkley Publishing Group,
200 Madison Avenue, New York, New York 10016.
The name "ACE" and the "A" logo
are trademarks belonging to Charter Communications, Inc.

PRINTED IN THE UNITED STATES OF AMERICA

10 9 8 7 6 5 4 3 2 1

From the team that brought you the other two—here is the
third in the Jake Cardigan Series.

The Team

—Ron Goulart	Center
Carmen LaVia	Right Guard
Lisa Wager	Left Guard
Ivy Fischer Stone	Right Forward
Susan Allison	Left Forward
Fifi Oscard	Referee

Keep playing, team, we're going to the Championships!

*This work is dedicated to
Marcy, Leslie, Liz, and Melanie,
with a small thank you to Grant,
and a large one to Mary Jo.*

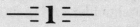

— ⹀1⹀ —

THE KILLER WAS carrying two weapons. One
was a stungun, the other a lazgun.

It was two weeks before Xmas in the year
2120. In the narrow alleys and passways between the towering apartment complexes
along the Seine in Paris seasonal carols were
being piped out of compact floating speakers
shaped like tiny golden-haired angels. The
hour was close to midnight and a thick fog was
drifting in off the chill river. The small fluttering wings of the overhead angels were speck-
led with mist.

A short, thin man of forty, staggering some,
was making his way along one of the twisty,
foggy lanes. His expensive suit was rumpled
and he kept one hand pressed against the damp
plazbrix of the nearest wall as he glanced
around. On his pale, perspiring face both anxi-
ety and puzzlement showed. He appeared to be

lost in the deserted passway, confused as to how to find his way home.

He slowed his pace, feet shuffling.

As he moved beneath one of the small singing angels, its mechanism suddenly expired. Song dying, it lost power and fell, hitting him on the left shoulder and then crashing to the damp pavement.

The man, mumbling to himself, halted. Squatting, he attempted to pick up the fallen angel. His fingers missed on the first scoop and, losing his balance, he went sprawling out on the ground.

The killer appeared behind him, materializing out of the thick night fog. He was young, didn't look more than twenty-one or twenty-two, tall and lean. He had short-cropped hair, a bushy moustache, and dangling from his left ear was an earring fashioned from a Brazilian coin. He was dressed in a tattered, blood-stained uniform. It was the kind that had been worn by the United Nations Combat Forces during the Brazil Wars years ago.

He carried the stungun in his left hand, the lazgun in his right.

The small man became aware of him. He'd been able to push himself up out of his sprawl and was attempting to stand.

Grunting, he managed to struggle to his feet. He swayed, started to turn.

The killer fired his stungun.

The man rose up on his toes, made a few

broken, fluttering motions with his arms, then toppled forward. He hit the wet paving hard, facedown.

Easing slowly closer, the killer stood over the fallen man. He used his lazgun now, very carefully and precisely, to inscribe a huge X on the body. That, very efficiently, chopped it into four chunks.

Some of the spurting blood dotted the white wings of the broken angel, some of it splashed across the toes of the killer's boots.

Genuflecting beside the remains, he jerked a note out of a pocket in his ragged tunic. He fixed it to one of the pieces of the body, a left arm and part of the torso.

The handprinted note said—"This is for Brazil! (Signed) The Unknown Soldier."

"Jesus," observed Sid Gomez.

"Yeah, exactly," agreed Jake Cardigan.

It was thirteen days before Xmas, and an artificial snow was falling all across Greater Los Angeles, part of the seasonal special effects. Up in Tower II of the Cosmos Detective Agency Building, Walt Bascom, the chief, had been showing a holographic simcast to Jake and his partner. The computer-generated projection was based on data gathered by the agency, plus information provided by various law enforcement agencies.

Bascom, a modest-sized man of fifty-six, was rocking in his lucite rocker a few feet from the now empty oval projection stage. He was fiddling with something deep in the left-hand pocket of his coat, making more wrinkles and rumples in his already rumpled and wrinkled suit. "What we've just seen, gentlemen, is a re-creation of the slaying of our client's husband." He nodded toward where the simcast had unfolded. "The earlier killings in this series also—"

"Who's the client?" Jake interrupted.

"Her name is Madeleine Bouchon. I will give you a file with all the background information available to us up to this point."

"And her husband?"

"He was Joseph Bouchon, a former French diplomat who was currently—"

"But nobody actually saw Bouchon being killed?" Jake was a good-looking man, just a year from being fifty. He had a world-weary, weather-beaten look and sandy hair. "What we just watched was really a computer's pipe dream."

"Well, partially, Jake. But there was somebody up in a window who got a glimpse of the murder as it was taking place."

"And didn't bother to make any fuss or try to stop it?" Gomez looked disgusted.

"Most people seeing a serial killer at work try to remain as unobtrusive as possible," remarked the agency head. "I might have ducked under something myself after getting a gander at this guy. This killing was brutal."

Gomez, a curly-haired man some ten years younger than his partner, shrugged and settled back in his rubberoid chair. *"Es verdad,"* he conceded.

"This killing seems to fit in with the previous eight we're attributing to this murderer," continued Bascom, rocking more slowly. "They commenced a shade less than two months ago. The first one took place, appropriately enough, in Rio de Janeiro, and from there the Unknown Soldier started moving across the world, following an itinerary that so far only he understands."

"He's hit Panama, Manhattan, Lisbon, Madrid and other choice locations," Gomez commented.

Jake was leaning against a viewall, arms folded, his back to the false snowfall. "From what I've heard, most cops around the world seem to think this pattern killer is a deranged veteran of the Brazil Wars."

"It's certainly plausible," said Bascom. "Since most of the victims, including Bouchon, had at least some sort of connection with those wars."

"This simulated killer we just got through watching is supposed to be based on what few eyewitness accounts there are, right? Not only of this latest slaying, but of some of the earlier ones, too."

Bascom nodded. "That's right, Jake."

"But the killer we saw can't be a vet, crazed

or otherwise. The final 'Zil War ended nearly ten years ago."

"*Sí*," seconded Gomez. "This Unknown Soldier we just viewed can't be much older than twenty-two or so. They didn't have any twelve-year-old *soldados* down there—at least not on the UN side."

Bascom said, "Most law officials assume the man is extremely youthful looking for his age. None of the witnesses, keep in mind, got an up-close look at him."

Jake shook his head. "Something's not right."

"Indeed. Mrs. Bouchon is also of the opinion that certain aspects of her spouse's murder don't smell right," the agency head told him. "She's offering us a handsome fee to prove that her late husband was not eliminated by the Unknown Soldier."

"Handsome enough to provide Jake and me with a bonus?" inquired Gomez.

Bascom studied the ceiling. "Possibly, Sid," he replied eventually. "At any rate, you two need to rush over to Paris right away and find out who really did kill Bouchon. We've got you booked to leave from the GLA Skyliner Port tonight."

"Tonight?" Jake was frowning.

"With a tricky case like this one, and an extremely anxious client, getting to the crime scene with alacrity scores big points. Sometimes bonus points."

"I figured we'd leave in the morning," said Jake. "That way I can get up to Berkeley tonight to say goodbye to Beth Kittridge."

"I can depart for Paris tonight alone, *amigo,*" offered Gomez. "You can spend the night on fond farewells and join me over there *mañana.*"

Bascom had begun tapping his fingertips slowly on the arm of his chair. "Ever since you joined the outfit, Jake, I've tried to accommodate your personal life," he said. "But, you know, the Cosmos Detective Agency isn't primarily dedicated to rehabilitating troubled ex-cops who are trying to rehabilitate themselves."

"Nope, you're right," said Jake. "I don't want too many special favors. We'll both take off for Paris tonight, as scheduled."

"Bueno," Gomez said with a smile.

$=\mathbf{2}=$

"Xmas," muttered Jake sourly.

" 'Tis the season to be jolly," remarked Gomez, "or so I hear. But you sure ain't, *amigo*."

"I'm not," agreed Jake.

They were flying across twilight GLA in an agency skycar, through the simulated snowfall, toward the Skyliner Port in the Ventura Sector.

"We're embarking on a trip to Paris," reminded his partner, relaxing in the passenger seat. "That should cheer you up. Or is it that you hate to leave home and loved ones at such a festive time of year?"

"C'mon, Sid, you know that what few loved ones I have are scattered hither and yon."

"Beth Kittridge is only up in NorCal, in Berkeley. That isn't all that hither."

"Her I'm going to miss," said Jake. "I really wanted to see her tonight."

"You could've told Bascom to go to hell. He'd have backed down."

"No, that's really not the way to do things. Asking for special favors—that's something you get away with when you're a young hotshot."

"Even middle-aged hotshots like us deserve a few perks."

"Once we get settled on the skyliner, I'll just call Beth on the vidphone."

"A poor substitute for an in-person encounter."

"Yeah, lately I seem to be having most of my meetings secondhand, usually over the vidphone," said Jake. "Now that my son's in England, I only see him on the damn phonescreen."

"Listen, *amigo,* England is only a small jump away from Paris," reminded his partner. "Once we clear up this new case in our usual speedy and impressive manner, why you can hop over and visit Dan at his posh private school in the British countryside."

"You know, I'm not at all happy about what's been going on lately," said Jake. "I didn't like Kate's moving over there three months ago and dragging Dan along."

"Ex-wives—and I ought to know—have a tendency not to behave nicely," said Gomez. "At least Kate didn't bop you on the *cabeza,* the way my former first wife did just prior to leaving my conjugal bed."

"I'm glad Kate's back in good health." Jake punched out a landing pattern on the dash. "It's just that I don't believe she went to London for the reasons she claims."

"OK, I grant you the notorious Bennett Sands was transferred from a prison facility in NorCal to one in the British Isles. That doesn't mean he's going to be seeing your ex-wife once again."

"Sands got switched to England because supposedly that's the best place to get fitted for an artificial arm to replace the one he lost during that Tek raid down in Mexico a few months back." Jake frowned. "Maybe that part's true, but I tend to doubt that he had to be moved."

"The *hombre* is a busted Teklord, Jake. He doesn't call the shots anymore."

"I wonder. Sands was rich, still has lots of money stashed here and there."

"You really think he's in England for some other reason?"

"Yeah, I do. And the fact that Kate's there too isn't a coincidence."

"Has he got enough influence left to rig a prison break?"

Jake shrugged. "If he does and wants to run off with my erstwhile wife, that's fine," he said. "But, damn it, if they involve Dan, I—"

"Calm yourself, *amigo*," cautioned Gomez.

Their skycar was drifting down through the snowy afternoon. "Dan's school isn't that far from the prison where they're keeping Sands," said Jake.

"Well, they've got to put schools someplace. I know that people complain—they don't want schoolkids in their neighborhood."

"Another thing. Sands' daughter is over in England too."

"She's about the same age as Dan, isn't she?"

"Year or so older."

"Ah, a year can be an enormous gap when you're that age," said Gomez, sighing. "I recall once, down in the San Diego Sector, when I was a mere sprig of eighteen. I was warned off an older woman of twenty, who possessed a lovely set of—"

"His daughter's being there isn't a coincidence either."

"Daughters like to be in the vicinity of their pops sometimes."

"Why in this instance, Sid? He can't have any visitors at a maximum security facility like the one he's in."

Gomez settled further into his seat. "I think mayhap you're making too much of the geographical proximity of these folks."

"Could be I am," acknowledged Jake. "Dan and I, though, were starting to get along better. Then Kate hauled him over there to England."

"Look on the bright side," said Gomez.

"You'll probably be seeing him again in a few days."

"I don't want him getting hurt. Not, damn it, over something Kate does."

Their skycar, after slowly circling a Skyliner Port landing area twice, settled down and landed.

"Suppose we chat about something more cheerful?" suggested his partner.

"Such as?"

"What kind of guy signs his name to his killings?"

The Skyliner Port was a large oval structure with four tiers circling a four-story-high centrum. Because of the holiday season, festive sounds, smells, and colors were being pumped through various outlets. Jingling bells could be heard, mingled with the voices of youthful carolers. The scents of hot eggnog and blazing yule logs were thick all around, and zigzags of green and red light were crackling high overhead.

Walking alongside Jake as they made their way toward a ticket kiosk, Gomez kept busy rating the row of soliciting charity robots who were ringing bells, rattling tambourines, and shaking money tins. "Legit, legit, bunco, bunco," he ticked off. "Bunco, legit, borderline, bunco."

Jake grinned. "I notice you didn't contribute to any of them, not even the legit ones."

"By the time I settle my current missus'
Xmas bills, I'll have to head down here with a
tambourine of my own, *amigo.*"

The skyport was crowded. Visitors were ar-
riving and departing, many of them laden with
brightly wrapped bundles of Xmas gifts.

Just beyond a tall decorative palm tree that
had been festooned with Xmas ornaments
stood a plastiglass kiosk. Jake strode up to an
empty slot to pick up their Paris tickets.

Gomez waited nearby, hands in pockets, and
glanced around. "What's wrong, *chiquita?*" he
asked, noticing a forlorn girl of about fifteen
with two large suitcases standing next to a
water-vending machine.

"Oh, nothing, really." She was pretty and
dark-haired. "Someone was supposed to meet
me and they're late."

"Maybe I can help you find—*Chihuahua!*"

The girl gasped, pressing her left hand to her
breasts. "What's happening?"

One of her suitcases had risen up off the
floor. After hesitating for a few seconds at
knee level, it went flying up toward the domed
ceiling.

"Telek," realized Gomez, staring upward.

Jake, tickets in hand, came running over.
"He's up on Level 3," he said, pointing. "I just
spotted him catching the suitcase. You go up
that ramp, I'll use this one."

"We'll retrieve your bag, *linda,*" promised

the curly-haired detective. Pivoting, he started dodging through the crowd.

Jake went sprinting up the ramp, weaving through travelers and porterbots.

The telekinetic thief, who'd used his psi powers to levitate the suitcase from the first level up to the third, was elbowing his way toward an exit door by the time Jake caught up to him.

"Let's have the suitcase," called Jake, closing in.

"Skarf yourself," the telek replied. He was a gaunt young man, wearing somebody else's dirty white suit. About thirty years old, he had a grinning skull tattooed on his forehead in livid purple.

He lunged suddenly, pushed through the white metal door of the men's room.

Jake followed.

The first thing Jake noticed was that the robot attendant was lying flat out on his back on the white plaztile floor. A thread of gray, acrid smoke was drifting up from his dented skull.

The telek, smiling, was by the far wall. He was sitting on the stolen suitcase.

Standing beside him was a large, thick man in a sea-blue suit. He had a gun in his right hand. "Figured you'd take the bait, Cardigan," he said, chuckling.

— ≡3≡ —

THE BIG MAN with the lazgun said, "We don't necessarily have to kill you, Cardigan."

"That's comforting." He came a few steps farther into the room. "Who the hell are you?"

"Just a messenger boy."

The telek, sitting hunched on the suitcase, snickered.

The big man continued. "The message is this—you and your greaser partner don't want to go to Paris. No, shit, no. You guys want to stay right here in GLA where it's safe."

"Who's sending me this advice?" He took another step ahead, coming nearer to the sprawled white-enameled robot.

"Oh, just somebody who's interested in your health and well-being," he answered. "If you ignore this friendly warning—then trust me, you're probably going to have an accident."

"Yeah, an accident." The telekinetic thief snickered again.

"You might for instance lose an arm." The gunman gestured with his weapon. "I might, you know, slice the damn thing right off. That'd be painful, but it would sure as hell keep you from wandering off to Paris. So what we have—"

"Hey, I'm not anxious to shed an arm." Jake sounded uneasy, a little frightened. "C'mon, we can talk this over and work something out." He started, nervous eyes seemingly on the gunman, toward him.

"Look out for the bot, asshole!" warned the telek.

Jake tripped over the spread-eagled attendant. He fell, turned in midair, landed on his left side, and went scuttling across the slick white floor in the direction of the row of silvery sanair nozzles.

When he came to a stop, his stungun was in his right hand.

He fired and the beam took the gunman square in his broad chest before he could swing his lazgun all the way around to take aim at Jake.

The big man made an angry gulping noise, started shivering violently. His gun fell to the floor as he went toppling backwards. Unconscious, he slammed into the swinging door of a toilet cell. He fell back into the cubicle, his head cracking against the metallic seat of the unit.

The telek jumped to his feet. Using his psi

power, he lifted the suitcase up off the floor and was about to send it hurtling into Jake.

"Naw, don't do that, *cabrón,*" advised Gomez, who'd come quietly into the room with his stungun ready.

He shot the telek.

The skinny man gasped, stiffened, sat. The suitcase fell, landing with a thump in his narrow lap.

"It's *muy triste,*" said Gomez, glancing around and then sliding his gun back into his shoulder holster.

"What is—getting ambushed in a toilet?"

"No, *amigo.* I mean it's very sad being set up by that sweet little *niña* downstairs. She looked so innocent."

"They usually do." Nodding, Jake added, "Let's turn these goons over to the cops. We have a skyliner to catch."

"Any notion why they wanted to maim you?"

"Somebody doesn't want us in Paris."

Gomez laughed. "They don't know you very well," he observed. "Warning you to stay away is the surest way to get you to go there."

A robot in a Santa Claus suit was circling the satphone lounge of the Paris-bound skyliner, handing out eggnog. When he reached Jake's alcove, he said, "Merry Xmas, sir. Compliments of TransNip Skyways." He held out a steaming plazmug.

"Scram," suggested Jake, returning his attention to the ballheaded robot whose fuzzy image was flickering on the phonescreen he sat facing.

"Ho ho ho." The robot Santa moved on.

"Ah, here's the problem," said the bot on the screen, giving himself a whack in the temple as he arrived at an insight. "Miss Kittridge, you see, has a government monitor on her vidphone and therefore we—"

"I already gave you the bypass code number."

"Right, yes, so you did."

"So put through the damn call."

"Xmas season got you down, too? You'd be surprised how many customers we get this time of year who are grouchy and—"

"The call."

The robot vanished. Blackness replaced his image, then random spurts of rainbow light.

All at once Beth, slim and pretty, appeared with great clarity. "Jake—where are you?"

"En route to Paris," he explained. "Didn't have time to call you until now."

"You're working on a new case for Cosmos?"

"Yeah. And according to Bascom, an important one. Otherwise I'd be in Berkeley now instead of midair."

She smiled gently. "I miss you, too," she told him. "This duty stuff can really foul things up. What sort of job is it?"

"You've heard of the Unknown Soldier."

"Wait now, Jake," she said, frowning. "Your client must be Madeleine Bouchon."

"She's the one. You know her?"

"Yes, I do. Her husband was a top official with the International Drug Control Agency for the past five years or so."

"Six years. I just read the Cosmos file on him," said Jake. "You've met him?"

"Yes, sure. Because of my father's work, we got to know quite a few people connected with the IDCA."

"Before he joined the agency office in Paris, Bouchon was the French ambassador to Rio," said Jake. "He was there during the final months of the last war."

"Which means he could possibly have done something that caused the Unknown Soldier to put him on his list."

"That's true, but—"

"But there are also lots of people in the Tek trade with reasons for wanting him dead," Beth said, finishing Jake's thought.

"Madeleine Bouchon apparently thinks this was a copycat kill, with somebody using the Unknown Soldier's style to cover their murder." Jake slouched some in his seat. "It's possible I'm not the right operative for this case, since I suspect the damn Teklords of being responsible for almost everything that goes wrong around the world."

"A good deal of the time I suspect they've also corrupted my father."

"Things aren't getting any better now that you've been working with him again?"

"Ever since what happened down in Mexico—well, I simply don't trust him completely anymore," she replied. "But when those various and sundry government agencies started pressuring me to rejoin him so that the last phase of his work could be speeded up—Jake, I just found it impossible to say no."

"I know, since I went through most of it with you."

"Most of it but not all," she said quietly. "Lots of my most difficult debates went on inside my head. Anyway, I finally let myself be persuaded. You know that the hardest part was leaving you and GLA for a while and moving up here to work at the lab they've set up for my father. Tek is a dreadful thing, and if I can help wipe it out—well, that's an accomplishment."

"How close is his anti-Tek system to being ready to use?"

"We're very close," she said. "It should be soon."

"I'd better sign off now, Beth," he said reluctantly. "This doesn't look to be my best Xmas."

"We'll make up for it," she promised him.

After her image had faded from the phonescreen, Jake sat in the alcove watching the dead phone for nearly a minute.

The robot Santa returned, started to offer him a mug of eggnog and then thought better of it.

In England the snow was real.

All across Barsetshire a thick, silent snow was falling. By dawn the moorlands surrounding Maximum Security Prison #22 lay under a foot or more of fresh snow and a sharp wind was whistling around the high neostone walls.

One of the forcefield barriers that isolated the hospital wing from the rest of the prison buildings was malfunctioning slightly. It sputtered every now and then, making harsh crackling sounds in the thin gray dawn.

A door in the slick gray wall of the Hospital Complex hissed open to let three squat, wheeled robots come rolling out. They sped to the nearest forcefield transmitter and began making repairs.

In the second-level doctors' lounge two android medics were sitting silently in straight-back metal chairs, absently watching the repair work.

The only human in the gray room was a lean, dark-haired woman of forty. Wearing a two-piece medsuit, she was standing near one of the high, narrow viewindows with a plazmug of nearcaf clutched in both hands. After taking a sip of her nearcaf, she again glanced up at the floating clock.

Nodding to herself, she finished drinking,

tossed the empty cup into a bin. After checking
the time once more, she crossed the quiet room
and stepped out into the corridor.

A white-enameled nursebot was going by,
carrying a yellow plaztray with two doses of
medication on it.

The lean woman caught up with the robot
and casually patted her on the side. "Keep up
the good work, Sophie."

"Thank you, Dr. Dumler, ma'am."

The nursebot continued along the hall, then
walked up a ramp to the next level of the
prison hospital. When she halted in front of
the door to Cell 302, the scanner mounted
above the number tag looked her over thoroughly.

"ID code," requested the voxbox.

"30/203/083."

The door slid open.

"Ah, Sophie." Bennett Sands was sitting in
the cushioned chair beside his bed. "As usual
it's a pleasure to see you."

"Thank you, Mr. Sands, sir."

Sands was thin, thinner than he'd been a
year ago, and his face was pale. The deep shadows under his eyes were dark and sooty. He
had one arm. "You make this hole almost toler-
able," he said as he picked up one of the small
cups from the tray and drank down the sea-
blue liquid it contained. "Ugh. Never can get
used to the foul taste."

"Sorry, Mr. Sands, sir." For less than thirty

seconds, as Sands took the bright orange stuff in the second little cup, the nursebot leaned closer to him. In a voice pitched so that only he could hear it she told him, "Bouchon dead. Stand by."

The parasite disk that Dr. Dumler had attached to the robot's side now disintegrated. It became a fine dust that would dissipate as the mechanical nurse continued on her rounds.

After the nursebot left his cell, Sands brought his only hand up to his face. Masking his mouth for a few seconds, he allowed himself a brief, unseen smile of satisfaction.

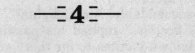

4

GOMEZ WAS RELAXING in their compartment when Jake returned from phoning. He was sipping an eggnog while he studied a yellow faxgram. "Is all well with Beth?"

"As well as can be expected." Letting out a disgruntled sigh, Jake settled opposite his partner. "Where'd you get the drink?"

"A robot decked out like Santa Claus came around giving them away. Even had a white beard. Very festive." He waggled the faxgram. "Bascom sent us some info on that pair of louts who tried to sandbag you. Care to guess?"

"Let's see . . . They're free-lance hoods," said Jake. "Got long criminal records. They don't know who hired them."

"Bingo." Gomez let the faxgram drop to the neowood table next to his chair. "Except you missed one point—they, both of them, have prior connections with Tek dealers."

27

"Yeah. I've been nurturing a hunch that there was going to be a Tek angle to this case."

"Whilst you were romancing Beth via satphone," said Gomez, "I've been rereading all this stuff the agency gave us on the Unknown Soldier murders."

"Commendable. Any insights?"

"Es posible," replied his partner. "Of the nine known victims so far there are three, including our Joseph Bouchon, who were currently tied in with anti-Tek activities of one sort or other."

"But they also had prior links with the Brazil Wars?"

"Sí, that tie-in is also there." Gomez paused to sample his drink again. "The fellow who was victim number 4—Colonel W. T. Reiberson, killed in Washington, D.C., late this past October—had trained jungle combat troops for the First Brazil War. The thing is, Jake, this *hombre* turned into a very vocal critic of the wars, started a stewpot of peace movements, and was eventually put out to pasture by the Army. At the time he was knocked off, he was managing an anti-Tek research facility just outside Baltimore. In fact, two of his top technicians were transferred out to Berkeley to assist on the Kittridge Project."

"Another connection with Beth's father," said Jake. "Joseph Bouchon and his wife were both friends of the professor and Beth."

Gomez took a long, thoughtful sip. "The

sixth victim was Dr. Francisco Torres, who got himself bumped off in Madrid the middle of November," he continued. "Now Torres did serve on the staff of a United Nations field hospital during the Second Brazil War, but that doesn't exactly make him a war criminal."

"Not to you, but a madman might look at it differently."

"Verdad. But this Torres had been running a scatter of rehab centers for Tek users since back in 2116. Initially, and until he fell from grace, none other than Bennett Sands provided about sixty percent of the operating funds for those centers from the impressive profits from his various legit business enterprises in Europe."

"Sands . . . Kittridge," said Jake slowly. "Okay—were there any discrepancies on any of these three killings? Details that don't exactly match those of the other Unknown Soldier murders?"

"The message tagged to Colonel Reisberson was worded exactly like all the others, and you know that the law boys around the world have never released the exact content of any of the notes. But—"

"We found out the exact wording, so could a copycat."

"That's what I'm coming to, *amigo,*" said his partner. "The lettering on the Reisberson note wasn't done by the same person who did the others. Wait, let me amend that. The other

29

notes look to have been lettered by some mechanical means—by a robot, an andy, or a secretary machine. None of them showed the characteristics of a human hand at work."

"Maybe the copycat didn't know that when he killed the colonel."

"Sí, but he found out sometime before he knocked off Torres," said Gomez. "If he did knock him off."

"Okay, suppose three of these damn killings are fake," said Jake. "If that's so, then we're talking about something much more complex than someone's killing Bouchon and trying to mask it."

"And behind that complexity, *amigo,"* said his partner, "the Teklords are probably lurking."

The highly polished bellbot carried their luggage into the second-floor hotel suite. "The Louvre Hotel has quite an illustrious history, messieurs," he explained, placing the three suitcases on a valet stand. "Though completely up to date in its modernity, it dates back to the twelfth century. Before the Louvre became a first-rate hotel, it was—"

"We know." Gomez wandered over to a wide window to gaze out at the simulated Tuileries Gardens that stretched away below in the overcast afternoon.

"Oui, this splendid place was once a famed museum," continued the robot, moving around

the living room to flip on switches and push buttons. "Then came the dread Panic of 2093 and our esteemed government was forced, alas, to sell all the art treasures it held and convert it into this—"

"We know." Gomez turned away from the arched window.

One of the things the bellbot had turned on was the vidscreen that occupied one wall. Three people were sitting in uncomfortable chairs and arguing with each other on the huge screen.

"That's none other than Professor Joel Freedon on the left there," Jake noticed. "The guru of the pro-Tek cause." He nodded at the thin man with the long, dead-white hair.

"I recognized him, *si.*" To the lingering robot Gomez said, "You can turn up the volume on that and then take your leave."

"Very well. *Adieu.*"

". . . Tek simply is *not* addictive," Freedon was saying. "In point of fact, Tek is a harmless liberating agent that frees the imagination, soothes the psyche that's been ravaged by the scourges of our so-called civilized mode of—"

"Repetition doesn't make lies any truer, Mr. Freedon," interrupted the heavyset woman sitting two seats over from him. "You know full well that Tek is indeed dangerously addictive. That in a far too high percentage of cases it also causes severe and irreversible brain damage. The incidence of epileptic seizures among Tek addicts has been growing—"

"Folk tales and fancies purely," dismissed the professor. "There does not exist one shred of reliable research to—"

"Perhaps," cut in the nervous young man in the middle, "if we were to return to some semblance of coherent debate we might—"

"This man is incapable of coherence."

"If *Doctor* Lance would simply attend to what I'm saying, and listen with her heart *and* her supposedly brilliant mind, she'd perhaps hear something new and wise. She might come to realize that she has simply been mouthing International Drug Control Agency propaganda and pap rather than—"

The three of them suddenly vanished. Replaced by a scene of fire and confusion.

"A special news bulletin," said a deep, excited voice. "Just moments ago here at the Central London Skybus Station an alleged major British Tek dealer—as yet unidentified—was assassinated. In addition to the alleged Tek kingpin, five apparently innocent bystanders were also killed. And fifteen—no, we've just been informed the toll has risen to seventeen—others were seriously injured. Police believe a kamikaze was used. As you know, a kamikaze is an android loaded with explosives. When the kamikaze makes physical contact with its intended victim, a tremendous explosion follows. In this tragic—"

Gomez turned off the wall. "Those Tek lads never grow tired of their tried and true tricks," he observed.

"Yeah, and they don't mind killing bystanders."

Gomez glanced around the living room. "I believe I'll freshen up and change before we drop in on our client," he announced. "Don't let in any exploding andies while I'm away."

The snow continued to fall in Barsetshire, England.

It flickered by the leaded windows in the main study hall of Bunter Academy.

Leaning closer to the black young man seated next to him at the long neowood study table, Dan Cardigan whispered, "What would you do, Johnsen?"

"I'd wait, old man. I'd sit on my butt, bide my time."

"But she's missing."

"You think she's missing," said Rob Johnsen while pretending to be gazing into his studyscreen.

"She's gone, nobody knows where she is."

"You're letting the fact that you're hot for Nancy Sands cloud your judgment, Cardigan."

"Listen, I've told you about her father and the way she's been—"

"Lots of girls have crooks for fathers."

"Ahum." A gray monitorbot had rolled over

33

to their table. It shook its metallic head nega-
tively. "Quiet, please, gentlemen."

"What about my request?" Dan asked the
mechanism.

"It's being processed, Mr. Cardigan."

"I asked for permission to make a call to my
dad early this morning."

"Your father is in America," reminded the
robot. "Overseas calls take time."

"No they don't."

"Overseas calls from Bunter Academy take
time," modified the monitorbot. "Now, gentlemen, I must ask you to refrain from further
conversation."

As soon as the robot had returned to its
place in the center of the large, beam-ceilinged
hall, Dan leaned and whispered to his friend,
"My father may be able to help."

"All the way from the United States, old
man?"

"He's a detective."

"Yes, I know, Cardigan. You've gone on at
great bloody length about him. The chap
sounds like a combination of Sherlock Holmes
and Sexton Blake."

"The thing is, I don't know if he'll have any
time to help me on this."

"Fathers, especially fathers who stick their
offspring into citadels of learning such as this
one, rarely have time even to return a call."

"No, he had nothing to do with my coming to
Bunter. That was all my mother's idea."

"Your mother's in England, isn't she?"

"Yeah, in London."

"Then maybe you ought to contact her about this."

"No, I can't do that," Dan said. "She used to . . . well, she's a friend of Nancy's father."

"All the better, old man."

"No, it's . . . I can't explain all that. But if I'm going to learn what happened to Nancy, I'll need my father's help," he said. "Or I'll just have to find her on my own."

Johnsen gave him a pitying look. "I really don't think, old man, that detective ability is inherited," he said. "Simply because your father happens to—"

"Mr. Cardigan." The robot had returned.

"Sorry, we'll quit talking."

"I've come to summon you. There's a vidphone call."

"Finally." He stood up. "From Greater Los Angeles?"

"No, from Paris."

While Gomez was in using the sonishower, Jake seated himself in the vidphone alcove in the living room. He put through a call to the dorms at the Bunter Academy in Barsetshire, England. He had to argue with three robots, an android, and someone who might've been human, and he had to raise his voice twice before his son finally appeared on the phone-screen.

"Hi, son. Gomez and I just got to Paris to work on a new case, and I wanted to hear how you're doing."

"I'm glad you called." Dan was a lean boy of fifteen, slightly taller and darker than his father. Right now he was looking worried and upset. "I've been trying to get hold of you."

"Is something wrong?"

"Not with me. What I mean, Dad, is this has nothing to do with how I'm getting along at this stupid school."

"I thought you told me you liked it at Bunter."

"Nope, what I told you was that this shithole is better than the shithole I used to attend in GLA. But please just listen a minute, will you?"

"Go ahead." Jake leaned closer to the screen.

"You remember my telling you that Nancy Sands was living near here?"

"Sure. You still seeing her?"

"Okay, I hear your disapproval in your voice," said Dan. "I realize you think her father is a crook. But Nancy's different."

"Let's hope so."

"Dad, Nancy's disappeared."

"Give me some details."

"For the past five or six days she's been acting . . . you know, strange. Women can be moody, I'm aware of that, but this was different. She's been really depressed and very nervous. Unhappy, too."

"About what?"

"She wouldn't tell me, but she hinted it was something pretty awful."

"Having to do with her father?"

"I think so, yeah."

"He's going to have a new arm fitted. It could be she's simply—"

"No. She told me last week she knows that the facility here is just about the best in the world for that sort of work."

"Okay. How long has Nancy been missing? And are you certain she really is missing?"

"She's been gone for over a day and, yeah, I'm damn certain," answered Dan. "Because one of those assholes came barging right into the school this morning to ask me if I knew where she was."

"Which asshole would that be?"

"Oh—Mr. McCay," answered his son impatiently. "He used to be a business partner of Bennett's. Ever since she came over here to England, she's been staying with McCay and his dumb wife in a big ugly mansion about ten miles from here."

"Has McCay gone to the police?"

"No. They're trying to find her first on their own."

"Did Nancy give you any hint that she was thinking of running away?"

"Not exactly."

"But?"

"Well, she has been talking about friends she knows in London."

"What does McCay think?"

"That I persuaded her to run away for some reason."

"He doesn't suspect that she may have been kidnapped or had an accident?"

"I asked him about that and he told me they were certain she'd taken off on her own."

"Then she probably left some sort of note."

"He says she didn't."

"He could be lying."

"Yeah, assholes do that," said Dan. "Dad, could you come over here and help find her?"

"No, we just arrived in Paris. I'm going to have to work here for a few days at least."

"But something may've happened to Nancy. Even if she did run away, it—"

"I'll contact a detective agency in London, Dan, one that's affiliated with Cosmos," his father promised. "They'll put an operative or two right on this. Okay?"

"Sure, I guess. But it would be a lot better if you could help out yourself."

"These ops are good, and they know England better than I do. Do you have a picture of her?"

"Lots of them."

"I'll tell them to get some from you."

"Should I go to the cops myself just to be on the safe side?"

Jake shook his head. "Wait on that," he advised.

"It's just that, you know, I want to be doing something."

"Get a detailed account of everything you know about her disappearance ready. One of the detectives will be contacting you and that'll help."

"I want to do more than that," said his son. "What's the earliest you can come over here?"

"Probably two or three days from now. But if there's an emergency, I can come right over."

"This is an emergency."

"I know you feel it is, Dan, but I don't think my boss would agree," Jake told him. "There's still a possibility, too, that she'll come home on her own. Runaways, it's been my experience, do that pretty often."

"No, I don't think Nancy will."

"Why not?"

"You didn't see her these past few days, the way she was acting, the way she looked."

"All right, hold on and I'll see you soon as I can." He gave Dan the number of the hotel. "Call me if anything new happens."

"I still wish you could. Okay, 'bye, Dad."

"Goodbye, Dan."

When Gomez, dressed in a new suit, came back into the living room a few minutes later, Jake was still sitting in the phone alcove, a thoughtful expression on his face.

5

THE CHROME-PLATED robot rose up out of his wrought-iron chair at the foot of the bright-lit gangway. Bowing smoothly, he reached up with his gleaming left hand and tipped his black beret to them. "Gentlemen?" he said cordially. His metallic right hand, which had swung up to waist level, had a lazgun built into the forefinger and a stungun in the thumb.

Gomez stepped closer, nodding at the large ivory-white houseboat that was anchored in the night Seine. "This would be the residence of Mrs. Bouchon, would it not?"

"Perhaps," replied the wide robot, right forefinger casually pointing at the detective's midsection.

"We're from the Cosmos Agency." Jake moved up to the foot of the gangway, putting himself between the guard and his partner. "We have an appointment with Mrs. Bouchon."

Smoothing his beret back in place on his slick, chromed head, the robot inquired, "You perhaps have identification, gentlemen?"

Gomez fished his ID packet from the pocket of his sky-blue suit. "That's a handsome boat Mrs. Bouchon dwells on," he observed as he passed over his identification.

"Oui," agreed the robot. A small rectangular panel in his chest opened and he held the ID to the gap. Lights flashed within, new whirs and hums were audible. "All in order."

After Jake had gone through a similar ritual, the guardbot stepped aside, tipped his black beret once again, and directed them to climb the gangway to the houseboat.

The boat was ornately decorated, thick with intricate neowood trim and looking more like a nineteenth-century villa than a twenty-second-century houseboat. There were hundreds of tiny glowing beads of white light worked into the trim on all three decks.

"Reminds me of the cake we served at my second wedding," remarked Gomez as they stepped aboard.

"It is quite gaudy, I know." A slim blonde woman of about thirty-five stepped out of a nearby cabin. "Joseph's tastes tended in that direction. I'm Madeleine Bouchon." She held out her hand.

"Jake Cardigan." He shook hands. "My partner, Sid Gomez."

When Gomez took her hand, he clicked his

heels, bent, and kissed the knuckles. "A pleasure, ma'am."

Smiling, the widow invited, "Join me in the conservatory," and led them along the highly polished deck into a large, glasswalled room. "One can see quite a way along the Quai Henri IV from here. If one is so inclined."

"Nice view." Gomez sat in a delicate wooden chair.

Jake sat opposite their client. "You don't think your husband was killed by the Unknown Soldier," he said.

"Ah . . . right to business."

Jake continued, "We've talked to the Paris police since we got here, and to someone in the IDCA office."

"Yes, and I'm sure they all told you that Joseph, coming home intoxicated from an Xmas party, was stalked and killed by that lunatic. Yes?"

Nodding, Gomez said, "They see it as fitting the pattern, Mrs. Bouchon."

"Do you feel then that this isn't worth looking into further?"

"No, we're here to investigate," Jake told her. "Supposing you start by telling us why it is you don't agree with everybody else?"

Madeleine Bouchon left the sofa she'd been occupying, crossed to a glasswall, and stared out into the night. "Is it the boat that unsettles you, Mr. Cardigan?"

Jake frowned. "Boat's fine. Lovely."

"Family money bought it. Joseph's family. I just live here." She turned to face him. "You may have the idea that I'm the usual spoiled rich bitch. But I'm not."

Jake reflected for about a half minute, then grinned. "Could be it is the boat," he said. "Excuse my churlishness."

"Let me explain that I was never deeply in love with my late husband," she said, returning to the sofa. "Yet I don't wish his murder to be covered up, for whatever reasons."

"Let's go over the things that bother you," Jake suggested.

"Would either of you care for a drink?"

Jake shook his head. Gomez said, "An ale maybe?"

Madeleine said, "Maurice?"

A small, tank-shaped headless robot rolled into the room. *"Oui?"*

"An ale for Mr. Gomez."

"Oui." The robot rolled over to where Gomez was sitting. Its drumlike chest popped open and it reached a mug off a shelf within. Holding its forefinger over the glass, it poured out foamy ale. *"Voilà!"*

"Gracias."

Jake waited until the wheeled robot had left them. "Okay, let's talk."

"For one thing, as I mentioned to Mr. Bascom, there was a witness who said she saw my husband staggering along the Boulevard Vincent Auriol a short time before his death,"

Madeleine said. "Joseph never drank, not at all, and he obviously never used drugs of any kind."

"The police suggest he'd been at a party."

"That's merely a supposition. There were, admittedly, several Xmas gatherings that evening that he might have gone to. Parties given by colleagues and friends. There's no evidence, however, that my husband attended a single one."

Gomez, after sipping his ale, inquired, "Where were you that night?"

"Home, here on the boat. As I already told your agency chief."

"You did, *sí.*"

Jake asked, "You think that witness is lying?"

"Perhaps. I think it more likely that Joseph *was* staggering, but that he'd been drugged somehow."

Gomez said, "You also told Bascom you thought your husband was going to be visiting a colleague that night."

"Joseph had been paying several visits over the past two or three weeks to a man who worked with him at the International Drug Control Agency office here in Paris," she said. "His name's Zack Rolfe."

Nodding, Jake said, "But Rolfe, from what we've been able to find out, says your husband didn't visit him that night. Or any of the other nights."

45

"Yes, I'm aware of that. Zack now claims that my husband has been having an affair with a young woman in the agency."

"Yeah, but Rolfe doesn't know who she is."

"Yes, exactly. Zack's story is that he was only doing my husband a favor by letting him pretend he was with him on all those nights. And obviously everyone seems to believe Zack."

"Did you ever try to phone your husband at Rolfe's?" asked Jake.

"No, because I never had any reason to. And Joseph didn't especially like to be interrupted during a business meeting, not unless it was a very serious emergency."

Jake said, "Rolfe's lying?"

"Obviously, yes."

"Why?"

"I don't know."

"How did you feel about Rolfe before this?"

"Joseph seemed to like him, and trust him." She shrugged gracefully. "To me Zack isn't the sort of man who causes strong feelings either for or against him."

"Perfect agency type," commented Gomez.

"My husband had been worried about something," said the widow. "For about the same length of time, I believe, that he'd been calling on Zack evenings. But, since Joseph had a strict rule never to discuss IDCA business with me, I have no notion what it was that was upsetting him so."

"And he didn't mention being worried about anything *outside* the agency?" Gomez finished his ale and set the glass on the floor.

"No," she replied, shaking her head. "He didn't tell me, if that's what you have in mind, that he was fearful the sins he'd committed during the Brazil Wars were about to catch up with him."

"Were there sins, ma'am?"

"No, there weren't," Madeleine replied. "At least I don't believe so. Joseph never discussed his days as ambassador to Brazil with me. All of that took place before we were married, you understand."

"If your husband *had* been seeing a woman," asked Jake, "would you have known?"

"Joseph wasn't interested in affairs of that sort, Mr. Cardigan," she assured him, smiling. "The work he was doing at the agency was what excited him."

"And, recently anyway, that was also what worried him."

"Yes. Whatever it was, it somehow ties in with the real reason why Joseph was killed."

"The police and his fellow IDCA agents don't agree," Gomez reminded her.

"And that," said the widow quietly, "may be another part of the puzzle."

—≡6≡—

GOMEZ, AFTER HE and Jake had separated to pursue different sources of information, strolled for a while along the brightly lit boulevards of nighttime Paris. He walked by a dozen or more sidewalk cafés, most of them operated by the Dutch conglom Bistros, Inc., and through three small hologram parks. When twenty minutes or so had passed and the curly-haired detective was completely certain that no one was tailing him, he made his way to the Boulevard Voltaire.

He paused beside a sidewalk stand where a chunky woman in her fifties was peddling plaz-flowers. Sniffing at a bunch of simulated yellow roses, Gomez studied the story-high illuminated archway across the street.

"You planning to buy those goddamn blooms, monsieur? Or are you just going to snuff all the smell out of them?"

49

"Ah, Marie, and here I thought you'd never forget me."

"Mon dieu! Gomez." Chuckling deeply, the heavyset vendor bestowed an enthusiastic hug on him. "You're in Paris."

"So I've been led to believe. How are you faring?"

"Better than you, judging from your appearance." Marie shook her head sadly as she scrutinized him. "Since I saw you two years ago, you've gotten paler and thinner. And you reek of cheap booze."

"I'm trim actually. And that's expensive ale, consumed purely and strictly in the line of business."

"You still a dick?" She tipped her head and smiled at him.

"I am, private now." He nodded at the arch across the way, which had the words METRO ESTATES written large on it in old-fashioned neon tubing. "Fact is, I'm planning on dropping in on our mutual chum, Limehouse."

Marie grunted. "That halfwit."

"Well-informed halfwit. He still living down in the estates?"

"Oui, he's down there, moldering away."

Gomez patted Marie on her broad back. "It's truly warmed my heart, *chiquita,* especially at this sentimental time of year, to encounter you once again." After slipping her a $10 Banx note, he went trotting across the street.

The arch rose up over a large hole in the

sidewalk. Two flashing arrows pointed at the broad stairway leading below.

Gomez paused to take a slow, careful look around, then headed underground.

Jake, meantime, dropped in at a Left Bank establishment known as the Hot Club. The club specialized in hologram and android re-creations of American jazz music of the twentieth century. On the ground level tonight Jelly Roll Morton and His Red Hot Peppers appeared to be playing on the small floating bandstand. There were less than ten patrons sitting at the small tables amidst the simulated smoke.

On the second level of the Hot Club Jake made his way through another artificially smoky room that held about fifteen customers. Art Tatum seemed to be playing an ivory piano in one shadowy corner.

Jake went through an arched doorway, climbed a curving ramp up to a heavy door marked CONTROL. He knocked twice.

Nothing happened.

He knocked again.

This time the thick metal door eased open a few inches. *"Oui?"* whispered a thin voice.

"It's Jake, Pepe."

"Jake who?"

"Jake Cardigan. We talked on the vidphone ten minutes ago."

The door opened a bit wider. "It does look like you, *mon ami.*"

"Well, that makes sense, Pepe. Since it is me. C'mon, let me in so we can talk."

The door opened even wider, enough to allow Jake to squeeze into the chill, dim-lit control room of the Hot Club.

Pepe Nerveux was a small, thin man, hollow-eyed and sharp-nosed. He had a tiny moustache that resembled a dab of lint and tight-curling gray hair. "Shut the door, please, quickly," he requested, rushing back to drop into his high, padded chair at his control boards. On the rows of monitor screens that rose up in front of Pepe Nerveux were dozens of images of what was going on in the five separate levels of the jazz club. Grabbing up an earphone, he tuned in on what Jelly Roll Morton's group was playing. *"Merde,* the trumpet's a shade sour." Anxiously, he reached up to twist a dial. "What do you think—is it better?" He held out the earphone toward Jake.

Ignoring it, Jake asked, "You implied on the phone that you're still in the information business."

"I am, *oui,* I am." Pepe Nerveux dropped the earphone, yanked a plyochief out of his trouser pocket, wiped sweat off his forehead, picked up another earphone. "No, non, *mon dieu!* They sent us a defective Cootie Williams for the Duke Ellington orchestra. Just listen to that dreadful mute work."

"You seem uneasy tonight," mentioned Jake, leaning against the wall.

"Supervising five jazz attractions, each of which has to be perfect, is stressful." He jabbed at a button on a control board at his right. "I'll have to dub in a new trumpet for the Ellington aggregation."

"Much more nervous than the last time we met."

"That was years ago, *mon ami*," reminded the small, narrow man, glancing briefly over his shoulder at Jake. "Keep in mind, too, that they call me Pepe Nerveux. That is not, obviously, my true name. No, it's a nickname, bestowed on me because I'm always very *nervous*. Nervous all the time, in fact. Ah, what's this?" He jumped up, gesturing unhappily at a row of monitor screens. "Bud Powell's fallen off his piano bench."

"I'm wondering, Pepe," said Jake, "maybe you're too busy to do business with me tonight."

"Wait, wait." He made a quick, shaky stay-put gesture with one hand while fooling with dials, buttons, switches. "*Bon,* he's back in place and playing 'Un Poco Loco.' " Sighing, Pepe Nerveux sank deeper into his chair.

"What about the background information on Zack Rolfe?" Cardigan persisted calmly.

"While his reputation isn't spotless, I haven't heard anything especially damaging about him. Since you called, I've instigated a further probe into his background." He tugged out his plyochief again, mopping fresh perspi-

ration from his face. "This evening, I just
learned, Rolfe is visiting the Grand Illusion.
That's a very swank electronic bordello not far
from here. A favorite spot of his." Pepe wiped
his forehead yet again. "Were you to drop in
there tonight, you might find out more about
him. Tell Madame Nana I sent you."

Jake said, "I'll maybe do that."

"My current fee for this sort of information
is $500."

"My current payout for this kind of information is $200."

"That is far, *mon ami,* from a fair price."

Jake handed him two $100 Banx notes. "You
want to be careful not to price yourself right
out of business."

"Very well." Pepe Nerveux gave a nervous
shrug. "Since we're old friends, I'll accept
what from another would be an insulting fee."
He snatched the bills. "Should you require
. . . *Merde!* Why isn't Jelly Roll on the stand?
He's not due to take a break yet."

"Thanks for your help." Jake left the control
room, walked back down through two levels of
the club and into the street.

He'd gone less than fifty feet from the doorway of the Hot Club when all hell broke loose.

=7=

THE AIRCIRC SYSTEM down in Metro Estates was
on the fritz and there was a foul, rancid odor
thick in the underground streets. Some of the
hologram projectors weren't functioning prop-
erly either. The wooded park on Gomez's left
as he walked toward Limehouse's cottage on
Downlevel 3 clicked off at irregular intervals.
The stately trees, pines, and some other kind
that Gomez couldn't identify, would abruptly
cease to be. Instead the stark metal walls,
smeared with fiery rust and pocked with blis-
tered paint, would appear, along with puddles
of scum-topped water.

When the grass snapped away in the simulated park, the body of a dead dog that had
been lying next to a plashing fountain remained, sprawled stiffly on the ribbed metal
flooring.

"Dog must be real," concluded Gomez.

"Stands to reason. Nobody'd consider a canine corpse decorative, not even down here."

A handsome Gothic church on his right began to quiver as he was strolling by. Instead of vanishing in an instant, as the grass and trees had, the narrow gray church seemed slowly, gradually, to melt. When it was nearly gone, and the spattered walls behind it were showing distinctly, the cathedral all at once reappeared and was whole again.

"Hallelujah," commented Gomez.

"You can help me, monsieur." A one-legged man came shuffling toward him, supported by a rough-hewn wooden crutch. He staggered, walking right through the wall of the newly returned cathedral.

Warily, Gomez slowed. "How?"

"All I need is skyliner fare to Australia. I got a job waiting there for me, but I'm a little short on my ticket money."

"How short?"

"Only $700, monsieur."

Gomez, smiling briefly, handed him a $10 Banx note. "Well, here's my contribution."

"Ten bucks? I sure as hell can't get to Australia on ten lousy bucks."

"It's a start though." Shrugging sympathetically, Gomez continued on his way.

"Jesus, I'm a vet, you know," called the beggar. "I lost my goddamn leg in Brazil."

Gomez kept moving.

"Looking for fun, curly?"

Sitting, legs crossed, on the porch of a two-story apartment building was a thin girl of about fourteen.

Gomez stopped. "Whatever you do, don't tell me a sad story."

"Who mentioned sad? Three hundred dollars." She smiled at him. She had almost all her teeth.

"For what, *chiquita?*"

"A night of fun. With me."

"How old are you?"

"How old do you like 'em?"

He gazed up at the black, shadowy metal ceiling of the tunnel for about ten seconds. "Waifs and strays," he muttered. "Especially at Xmas I seem to bump into them."

"If you act fast, curly, I'll drop the price to $200. And that includes a continental breakfast comes the dawn."

"Here." He leaned closer to the girl. "Here's $50. Now take it, go home, quit hustling for tonight."

"You trying to reform me?"

"A lost cause, huh?" He put the $50 Banx note in her thin, knobby hand. "Well, *adiós.*"

Shoulders hunched, he walked on.

"Too bad, curly," said the girl to his back. "You're sort of cute."

"She's right about that," he said to himself, kicking up his pace.

Limehouse was out in the small garden in front of his cottage, on hands and knees among the tulip beds. He was a long, thin man, somewhere between thirty and fifty. A cyborg with a right arm of tarnished silver. "Just the ruddy bloke I'm after wantin'," he said, noticing Gomez stepping over his low white picket fence.

"Como está?"

"Can't complain, m'lad. Now tyke a bloomin' gander art these 'ere tulips, will yer?"

"Momentito," cut in Gomez. "I know full well that you're a one-time Londoner, Limehouse, and that you're loyal to the Merrie Old England of bygone days, but, *por favor,* spare me that godawful stage Brit accent."

"Bit much, wouldcher say, gov?"

"A bit, *sí.*"

"It seems to please the tourists, you understand? Especially the ones who drop down here from Great Britain. You really, you know, can't spread it on too thick for them."

"You had a query?"

Creaking some, Limehouse got up out of the tulip beds. "Take a long appraising look at these tulips if you will. Then tell me if you can tell which ones are the real article and which are simply projections."

Gomez scanned the rows of bright flowers. "Red ones are phony."

Limehouse sagged. "How'd you bloody tumble to that?"

"Your projector's on the blink. The flowers

on the end keep fading away until you can see
through them."

Crouching, he scowled at the red tulips. "Ar,
blimey, you're absolutely right. My eyes aren't
as sharp as they ought to be, and that's for
certain."

"Might we step into your parlor for a chat?"

"Sure thing." The cyborg led him into a cozy
parlor, where a small cheery fire seemed to be
blazing in a rustic stone fireplace. "Sit yourself down. Tea?"

"Not at the moment."

Settling into an armchair, Limehouse
rubbed at his metal arm with the fingers of his
flesh hand. "I've been making discreet inquiries since you called me this afternoon."

"With what result?"

Poking his fingers into a pocket of his checkered vest, the cyborg extracted a small vidcaz.
"I was able to acquire a copy of this," he said
as he inserted it into a slot in his arm. "It's not
complete, mind you, only about two minutes
long. The interesting thing, though, is that
this particular bit of footage isn't in the official autopsy video on your late friend, Joe Bouchon."

"Roll it." Gomez dragged his chair closer to
that of his host.

Limehouse opened his metal hand to reveal
a small vidscreen built into the palm. When he
twisted his metal thumb, a picture appeared on
the screen.

"Oy," remarked Gomez, grimacing.

Lying on the white medtable were the four portions of Bouchon's body. An android medic in a bloodstained smock was standing beside the table talking to a white-enameled robot who was holding a tray of liquid-filled vials.

Limehouse twisted his forefinger and voices came out of the tiny speaker below the screen.

". . . no alcohol?"

"None, sir," replied the white bot.

"What did you find?"

"He'd been given, orally, a dose of vertillium. Approximately a half hour before he died."

"Hmmm," said the android thoughtfully. "What about—"

The film ended.

"Vertillium," Limehouse started to explain, "is a fairly powerful—"

"Disorienting drug, sí. I'm familiar with the stuff." He slid his chair back a few feet. "Do you know who edited this snippet out of the official version of the autopsy?"

Pointing at the ceiling with his silver thumb, the informant replied, "Somebody important. Don't know who."

"Find out."

"Might be expensive."

"I've got a good budget."

"It could also, Gomez, be dangerous. To the both of us."

"I'd appreciate it, nonetheless, if you'd try,

in your celebrated discreet and polite fashion," urged the detective. "Do you have anything else for me?"

Limehouse coughed into his real hand.
"What I've supplied you thus far I'd like to
have $1000 for."

"Fair enough."

"There is something else." His voice lowered. "But on this I don't happen to be the sole
proprietor. If you want it, the whole story is
going to cost you an extra $1500."

"Who's your partner?"

"Don't explode when I tell you."

"I'll make every effort not to."

"It's Eddie Anguille."

"Shit."

"Eddie came to me when he got wind of what
I was scrounging around for."

"That *cabrón*. If they gave out trophies for
swinishness, Anguille would cinch permanent
possession. If they took a poll to determine the
ten most unreliable and untrustworthy louts
on the face of the earth, he'd fill the spots from
one to five. Maybe six, too."

"I don't especially favor the bloke myself,"
admitted Limehouse. "But he's got this and if
you want it—well, sir, it's $1500."

"Do I get a sample of what I'm buying?"

"I have a bit of audiovisual material, yeah. A
conversation snippet about a certain artifact
as it were," explained Limehouse. "However,

Gomez, to really find out what it all means, you got to go to Eddie."

"In what pesthole does he hang his hat these days?"

"The Hotel Algiers."

Nodding, Gomez said, "A first-class dump for sure. Is this sample going to cost me extra?"

Rubbing his metal hand along his leg, Limehouse said apologetically, "If it was up to me, you understand, I'd run this off for you for nothing. But Eddie, he doesn't believe in free samples."

"What's the tab?"

"Two hundred fifty."

"Plus the $1500 when I go to him?"

"That's the blooming deal, I'm afraid, Gomez."

"You don't usually work cons."

"This isn't a scam. Leastwise I don't think so."

Gomez left his chair. On one wall of the parlor hung portraits of past and hopefully future kings and queens of England. "Queen Victoria looks a trifle sexier than she did in my history class at high school."

"The artist, I expect, took a few liberties. What do you think of the latest portrait I've added?"

"Which one?"

"On the end of the lower row."

"King Arthur II? Who the hell is he?"

"He'll perhaps be the king of England someday." Limehouse stood up, enthusiasm spreading across his thin face. "By all rights he should be sitting on the throne of England even as we speak."

"There isn't any throne of England," reminded Gomez. "England's been a democracy since the revolution some sixty years back."

"That there was the worst bloody thing that ever happened to Great Britain." Limehouse sat down again. "Ousting the monarchy and putting in a president. I'll never set foot back home again until—"

"Okay, I'll take you and Eddie up on this deal," Gomez told him. "Here's the $250. What does that buy me?"

Limehouse showed him.

Jake heard the fight before he saw it.

Something was happening up in the narrow alley that ran alongside the Hot Club.

Someone cried out in pain. Then came the sound of a body slamming into the ground. A plazcan hit the pavement, spilled coins clattered.

"Don't, please."

Jake went sprinting to the mouth of the alley.

A flung crutch nearly hit him as he reached the opening. Dodging, he entered.

On the rutted pavement a ragged man in an old Brazil Wars jacket and a pair of suit trousers was screaming and thrashing around as two large young men in skin-tight black clothing kicked at his ribs and groin.

"What did we tell you, asshole?"

"Not to . . . ow!"

"What? Speak up, *cafard*. What did we tell you?"

"Not to . . . beg around here . . . ow ow."

"That's right."

Jake said evenly, "I think he's got the message, fellas. You can quit."

The larger of the two large young men stopped kicking the crippled beggar and took a step back. "This is none of your business, asshole."

"Skarf off," said the smaller of the two. "Or you're going to need a cup and a crutch."

"Quit," advised Jake quietly.

"Screw you." The larger one kicked the fallen man again in the ribs.

Jake moved fast. He caught the thug's left arm, twisted it behind his back. Spinning him half around, he shoved. The force of the push sent the man all the way across the alley to smack into the sooty stone wall opposite.

Jake nodded at the other thug. "Be a good idea to go away."

"Like hell, *cafard*." He came charging at Jake.

Jake sidestepped, kicking out.

The man howled as Jake's booted foot

smashed into his kneecap. Cursing, he stumbled and fell against his rising partner.

Watching them, Jake bent over the beggar. "Can you get up?"

The Brazil vet gave Jake a thin, sly smile. "Sure, Cardigan." He jumped to his feet.

The two others were already scurrying clear of the alley.

The beggar thrust a note into Jake's hand, ducked around him, and went running off.

The note said—"The beggar could have been a kamikaze. Go home to GLA."

= 8 =

THE ROBOT DOORMAN at the narrow five-story Hotel Algiers had broken down some time ago and fallen to the sidewalk. No one had bothered to pick him up or had attempted to repair him. Rusted, gutted, scrawled over with rude messages in several tongues, he lay on his back just to the left of the lobby entrance.

A cold, harsh rain had started to fall about a half hour earlier and it was hitting the carcass of the doorman, making loud pinging noises. The cracked paving was slick and black.

Gomez's skycab came sputtering down through the rainswept night, dodging between the multilevel pedramps that skirted the hotel and the other rundown buildings in this forlorn section of Paris.

Hopping clear of the jittery cab as soon as it touched down, Gomez ran into the Algiers, skirting the fallen doorman.

"Madre," he commented as the foul odors that had collected in the small circular lobby assailed his respiratory system. The scent of unwashed flesh predominated, but the detective also noted spoiled food, urine, dead rodents, strong antiseptics, and dying flowers.

The clerk, a fat black cyborg, was slumped over the simulated-marble desk. His copper right arm dangled over the edge.

Narrowing his eyes, Gomez studied him. "Ah, he's breathing," he determined after a watchful ten seconds.

Finding his way to the stairway, he began his ascent. The elevator looked as though it wasn't to be trusted.

New odors hit him as he climbed toward the third floor, where Eddie Anguille had his room. Smokable drugs, vomit, something vile that he couldn't identify.

On the second floor landing of the venerable hotel Gomez nearly tripped over a discarded metal foot and ankle. "Careless," he mentioned, continuing upward.

The thin neowood door of room 383 had a triop photo of a naked woman pasted on it. Someone, long ago, had drawn shaky red circles around each of her breasts.

"Paris is still an art center, I see." Shrugging, Gomez tapped on the door just to the right of the naked woman's knee.

There was no discernible response.

He tapped once more.

68

Then he heard a faint rasping voice. "Who is it?"

"Gomez. Limehouse sent me."

"Who?"

"I'm Gomez. The gent who sent me is Limehouse."

"Minute."

Three minutes later someone scratched at the other side of the door. Another minute passed, the door creaked open.

"C'min, Gomez. I'm sick."

Gomez went in sideways, careful to avoid contact with Anguille, who stood swaying in the opening. He was small, not more than five foot four, and a grayish white color. He was wearing a soiled blue and white striped shirt, a pair of baggy shorts, and one sock.

On the little lame bedside table next to his gray unmade cot sat the evidence of a recent Tek session. There was a Brainbox, the roach-like Tek chips, and the electrodes to hook up the box to your skull.

"You've added Tek to your long line of vices, huh?"

Anguille started to reply, but began coughing instead. "Shit, Gomez, I'm not that stupid," he was able to say eventually. "Naw, that crap belongs to my girlfriend."

"And she's where?"

"Out."

"Sit down somewhere," suggested Gomez. "We'll talk business."

"You don't like me, never have."

"True, but you have some information I may need. Or so you told Limehouse."

Anguille's left leg suddenly went out on him. He slumped, listed to the left, staggered back, and dropped into a seated position on the rumpled cot. The room's only window was in the wall just behind the bed. It was missing a pane and the wet night wind was worrying at the splotched plyotowel that served as a curtain. Shivering, Anguille asked, "Do you happen to see my fricking pants around here anywhere?"

Gomez glanced around the dim room. "That might be them lurking under the chair."

"Yeah, that's them. Could you—I really am sick—could you fetch them for me?" asked the informant. "I don't like to sit around with my butt hanging out when I have company."

"You always were fastidious, Eddie." Gingerly, Gomez plucked the ragged pair of pants from under the lopsided chair and tossed them to Anguille. "Now tell me about that minute of conversation you passed on to Limehouse."

"He tell you my price?"

Nodding, Gomez dragged over the chair the trousers had been under. He was about to sit when he noticed a thick spill of something green and sticky on the seat. Pushing the chair aside, he said, "We'll discuss price after I find out if you have anything beyond what I heard and saw."

"I got more, sure." He was breathing with

difficulty as he attempted to tug on his pants while sitting on the cot.

Gomez looked away. "Very fuzzy bit of video. You claim the two gents conversing are with the Paris Police Bureau."

"They are, trust me. That piece you saw came from a much larger sequence," said Anguille, still struggling with his pants. "A colleague of mine made it for a different purpose altogether."

"For all I know," Gomez pointed out, "those two lads were also colleagues of yours pretending to be cops."

Wheezing some, Anguille finally got the pants all the way on. "No, it's a real police conversation, between two high-place officials," he swore. "And, what's important to you, Gomez, is that they're talking about the *other* letter from the Unknown Soldier."

"Not the note that was stuck to Bouchon's remains?"

"No, no, a different letter entirely. One that was sent directly to the cops."

"The Unknown Soldier never does that, Eddie. It's not his method."

"Well, he sure as hell did it this time. Once I happened to hear about what was said on this vidfilm—since I already knew why you were in town—I realized I was onto something," explained Anguille, breathing shallowly. "I made a special effort, Gomez, and busted my

71

ass for you. I got hold of a copy of the very letter."

"And that's what you're selling?"

When he nodded, Anguille set himself to coughing again. "Right you are, for $1500."

"Why don't I just trot over to the police as an accredited operative and ask to see the damn letter? Be cheaper."

"The reason you can't do that, Gomez, is because they won't admit that they have such a letter. You heard them talking about covering it up."

"What's bothering me," said Gomez, "besides the godawful smell of this room, is what I know about your past activities. You're not, Eddie, the most trustworthy gent in Paris."

"Look, you can have it for $1000," offered the ailing informant. "I happen to be in need of quick cash. And, shit, I laid out $500 for the damn letter myself."

Nodding, Gomez told him, "Okay, it's a deal." From his jacket pocket he took out the $1000 in Banx notes that he'd slipped in there earlier. "Where's the letter?"

Anguille lifted his backside off the bed. "In my pants. That's why I was so anxious over them." He reached into a hip pocket and came out with a folded sheet of faxpaper. "You hand me the money and I'll—holy shit!"

He stood up completely, staring at something behind Gomez.

Spinning around, Gomez was just in time to

see the door of the little room begin to crumble away to dust.

Jake stepped out of the Parisian night and into the Grand Illusion bordello, from the rainy ped-ramp into the sultry simulated formal garden. Paths of spotless white gravel crisscrossed what appeared to be acres of well-cropped bright green grass. There were rows of rose-bushes in full scarlet flower, great topiary hedges carved into the shapes of crouching panthers, roaring lions, and running wolves. There was a tall fountain up at the center of the holographic garden, topped with a lifesize statue of a naked young woman pouring deep blue water from an urn. The steamy scent of hothouse flowers was thick in the air.

Sitting in a white metal chair in a pink arbor near the fountain was a black young woman dressed in a delicate nineteenth-century gown. On the white metal table beside her rested a portable vidphone.

The gravel crunched underfoot as Jake made his way over to her.

"Evening," he said when he reached the arbor.

"Good evening, sir," she said, smiling pleasantly. "My name is Onita and I'm your receptionist for tonight here at the world-famous Grand Illusion. Before we proceed with satisfying your every sexual need, I am obliged by French law to inform you that, while I am a living, breathing human being, none of the hookers whom you'll encounter during your enjoyable stay here are real. Some are state-of-the-art androids, while others are simulated directly in your brain, using completely legal brainstim techniques. While we insist on a simple, painless robophysical exam for each and every customer, we accept no legal or moral responsibility for any subsequent physical or mental mishap that may befall you during or after you've indulged your passions at our establishment. If you have heard and thoroughly comprehended all this, please signify by saying yes."

"Yeah. But what I actually—"

"The next matter to settle, sir, is how you intend to pay for your evening's pleasures," continued the young woman. "While we prefer Banx notes in advance, we do honor Wurld-Kard, DisneyCharge, and—"

"Onita, I'm not a customer."

"If you're suffering from financial difficulties, sir, our friendly Loan Department stands ready to—"

"What I mean is, I really came here to talk to Madame Nana."

"She never sees any—"

The vidphone chimed discreetly.

"Excuse me, sir." She turned the phone so Jake couldn't see the screen. "Yes, ma'am?"

"Is that Jake Cardigan?" inquired a slightly harsh female voice.

"Are you?" asked Onita, looking up at him. He nodded. "I am, yep."

"I thought so," said the phone. "Send him right up to my suite, honey."

"Yes, ma'am." Hanging up, she smiled more brightly at him. "Madame Nana wishes to see you, sir. Are you a celebrity?"

"A nonentity, really. Where do I find her?"

Onita pointed. "Go along this path until you come to the tiger hedge. Turn right on that path and when you come to the arch of wild flowers, stop and wait. An escort will come for you. You sure you're not someone I might have heard of?"

Jake grinned. "That seems unlikely," he told her. "But then I don't know what sort of people you hang out with in your off hours."

He started on his way.

—— 9 ——

As THE FIRST husky hoodlum stepped through the opening where the hotel room door once had been, Gomez tossed the sticky chair across the room at him. Then, ducking low, he spun and dashed toward the cot. While jamming his Banx notes back into his pocket with one hand, he snatched the sheet of folded paper out of Anguille's knobby hand.

The first hood, propelled by the legs of the chair nudging him hard in the chest, stumbled backwards into the second hood, who was still in the shadowy corridor outside.

Gomez continued in motion, walking right across the unmade bed. He yanked aside the plyotowel that served as a curtain, went climbing through the paneless window. As he'd noticed when approaching the Algiers by skycab, there was a pedramp running close to the third-floor windows and about six feet below them.

He jumped free of the room, hitting the rain-slick ramp on his side. He skidded, rolled a few feet, came to a stop. He sat up and very rapidly tucked the copy of the Unknown Soldier letter away. Yanking out his stungun, he scrambled to his feet and glanced back up at the window.

"Gomez." Anguille was framed there in the light, trying to climb over the sill. "Help me."

"Stand aside so I can get off a shot."

The informant screamed then. The whole front of him, from neck to waist, seemed to explode out into the night. Fragments of flesh, bone, cloth came spurting all across the darkness.

Gomez started running away from there.

One of the two intruding hoods must have shot Anguille from behind with a needlegun, sending dozens of jagged darts into him.

As Gomez jogged along, concentrating on putting distance between himself and the Hotel Algiers, he noticed something up ahead on the rainy ramp.

Two more hoodlums, remarkably similar to those he'd left behind in Anguille's room, were standing there. Side by side, wide-legged, about a hundred yards away.

Halting, he took a quick look back over his shoulder. *"Chihuahua!"*

Another pair of goons was standing about two hundred yards to his rear.

This ramp was nearly three stories up from the street. So going over the railing and dropping down to ground level was especially impractical. Although he might be able to shinny down some of the fretwork.

"Shinnying while dodging four marksmen ain't going to be easy," he reminded himself.

The big louts up ahead, smiling, were leisurely drawing lazguns from inside their dark jackets.

He didn't bother to check behind him, since he was certain the other pair would be performing similar actions.

Gomez was about to try talking to them in a diplomatic fashion when he became aware of a sound growing up at his right.

He risked a glance.

A large skyvan was moving in close to the pedramp and seemed to be intending to land directly in front of him.

As the van lifted over the railing and started to set down, a stuncannon mounted atop its forward cabin swung around. A beam of orangeish light came sizzling out, hitting the two goons at his rear in turn. Each yowled, stiffened, and fell.

The words NEWZ, INC were emblazoned large on the side of the skycar, which was now hovering on the ramp between him and the two remaining hoods.

Gomez had a sudden suspicion as to who must be in the skyvan.

But when the door to the front compartment popped invitingly open, he didn't hesitate. He ran, zigzagging to make himself less of a target for anybody back at the hotel. He jumped right into the compartment.

This was better than getting shot.

Somewhat better anyway.

Madame Nana was long, lean, and dressed in tight black trousers and a black neoleather jacket. Her black hair was worn in a severe crew cut, she had a circular black patch over her left eye, and she was puffing on a thin, shriveled black cigar. "Hi, Jake," she said from behind her seethrough glass desk.

Her office simulated a sunlit forest clearing, and the big desk and the three glass chairs seemed to be sitting on grass and pine needles.

Jake stopped at the edge of the clearing to study the slim madam. "You've changed your name again, Lulu," he said finally.

"For business reasons."

"When I knew you in Greater LA six years ago, you were Madam Blueberry," he said. "And five years before that, down in Mexico, you called yourself—"

"No need to go back that far in time," she said. "Especially since everyone hereabouts thinks I'm thirty-one years old." She took a puff on the cigar, then exhaled a swirl of smoke. "Sit down, Jake."

He remained on his feet. "Though it's always a pleasure, I have to admit I dropped in on business."

"Please sit down. We're old friends and there's always time for pleasantries."

"My arresting you a few times for running illegal whorehouses in GLA doesn't exactly make us old buddies, Lulu." He lowered himself into a glass chair, watching her.

"Whenever you broke into one of my places because of some license trouble, you were always a gentleman."

He grinned. "That's not what you called me at the time."

"There's plenty of time for business. Tell me all about yourself." She leaned back in her chair and contemplated him. "I was sorry when I heard you got sent up to the Freezer for a fifteen-year stretch."

"I'm interested in one of your customers," cut in Jake. "Guy named Zack Rolfe."

"A friend and client, though a shade perverse in his tastes."

"I want to talk to him when he's through. Could you arrange an encounter?"

"That won't be a problem—and your timing is perfect, Jake," Madame Nana told him. "Zack likes to have a bit of supper first. Right now he's up in one of our private dining rooms with Felice, Paulette, and Rosco. I'll have one of my people take you there soon as we finish talking over old times."

Jake stood. "I'm about done."

"You haven't even told me how your old

pal's doing." She inhaled and exhaled smoke. "That horny Mexican—what was his name?"

"Gomez. And he's in crackerjack shape," said Jake. "Where's this dining room?"

"Gomez—yes. I should have remembered that. So do you ever run into Gomez these days?"

Putting both hands on the back of the glass chair, he leaned slightly toward her. "C'mon, Lulu. If I know you, you're already aware that Gomez and I work for the Cosmos Detective Agency and that we're in Paris on a case."

She flicked ashes off into the simulated grass. "You're thinking of me as I was during my Madam Blueberry days," she said. "These days, Jake, I concentrate on my business and take practically no interest in the outside world and its affairs."

"I'll pass your best wishes on to Gomez. How about that escort?"

Smiling, Madame Nana touched a panel at the edge of her desk. Chimes sounded off in the forest. "I'll have Marcel guide you up to the dining room. Sit down and rest until he arrives."

"How long is it going to take the guy to get here?"

"Not long. Five minutes."

It took nearly ten.

And another ten for the chrome-plated robot to lead Jake along dim-lit corridors and up gently curving ramps to the dining area high up in the Grand Illusion.

"Your friend Monsieur Rolfe is in Dining Room #13." Marcel stopped, bowed, pointed toward a wide pink door. "A discreet tap before entering is usually in order."

Jake was raising his hand to knock when a young woman screamed on the other side of the door.

═ 10 ═

THE REDHEAD SMILED at Gomez as he hooked himself into the passenger seat next to hers in the rapidly climbing Newz, Inc, skyvan. "I truly hope, Gomez, that you won't think I'm being overly critical of you, especially at a time such as this, when you've screwed up to such an extent that you very nearly got your backside in a sling and must therefore be feeling hugely disappointed in yourself and depressed by your manifest inadequacies, and it's all right with me, incidentally, that you haven't so much as bothered to give us even a teensy thank you for pulling your walnuts out of the fire or—"

"Chestnuts, Nat."

"Hum?"

"It's chestnuts that zealous folks are forever pulling out of the fire for other ungrateful folks." He slouched more deeply into the seat, watching the night rain hit at the window beside him.

"Be that as it may, and ignoring your grouchy reaction to what I myself judge to have been a really impressive hairbreadth rescue—"

"Didn't I tell you the fellow was a putz, princess?" A highly polished chrome-plated robot was piloting the skyvan. He had the words NEWZ, INC STAFF spelled out across his wide chest in diamond studs.

"Concentrate on your flying, Sidebar," cautioned Natalie Dent.

"I'm a cameraman, princess. I'm only handling this crate because the regular—"

"Don't get the idea, Sidebar dear, that I don't admire and respect you, even though I'm dead certain that the robotics firm that constructed you erred somewhere in the installing of your ego, but I do wish you'd refrain from interrupting me while I'm having a conversation with my old friend Gomez."

"A putz," reiterated the cameraman robot, returning his full attention to guiding the van through the rainswept Paris night.

Natalie patted Gomez on the arm. "Are you feeling okay?" she asked. "That spill you took would've jiggled a man half your age." She smiled sweetly.

"A man half my age would still be cooped up in a playpen," said Gomez. "What the hell brings you to Paris, Nat—and into such close proximity with me?"

"Well, as one of the ace investigative reporters in the profession and as a star newsperson for Newz, Inc, the top round-the-clock news service on video, I get a lot of plum assignments, and this alleged Unknown Soldier killing fits into the category of important stories," she replied. "It really strikes me as an incredible twist of fate that you and I are continually bumping into each other in these odd corners of the globe."

"Paris isn't an odd corner, Nat. Millions of people flock here daily."

"True, but I was just mentioning to Sidebar, right after we noticed you making your clumsy exit from Eddie Anguille's hotel room, 'It's funny how Gomez and I, while professing to have nothing in common, are continually showing up at the exact same spot.'"

Gomez straightened up in his seat. "You were en route to talk to Anguille?"

"Yes. Because I had a tip that he had a document that would bolster my theory about this particular killing," said Natalie.

"A document, you say, Nat?" Gomez assumed a guileless look.

"I'm referring to the letter sent by the Unknown Soldier."

"A letter, eh? Fancy that."

Sidebar snorted. "The letter you have in your pocket, putz."

"Sidebar, keep in mind that Gomez, even though he's being surly and is ungrateful about our saving him from surely meeting the same fate as poor Mr. Anguille and being splattered all over the side of that seedy hotel and on a goodly stretch of pedramp as well, is our guest and I won't have my pilot insulting—"

"I'm your cameraman, princess," corrected the robot. "Cameramen are notorious for their ready wit and backtalk."

"We've worked together admirably in the past," said Natalie, taking hold of Gomez's arm. "And, actually, it's as a person and not as a detective that I think you come up short. So there's no earthly reason why we can't work together again. It will save us both a lot of—"

"Lord knows, Nat, just seeing you again has inspired me with a whole new spirit of cooperation," he informed her sincerely. "The thing is . . . Princess—is it that they call you these days?"

"I dislike that nickname. Which Sidebar well knows, and that's, by the way, another indication that a major tune-up and overhaul wouldn't hurt him a darn bit. You can continue to call me Nat, which isn't all that attractive a diminutive, but since you can't bring yourself to use 'Natalie,' I'm willing to settle."

"Okay, Nat. The gratitude I'm feeling because of your timely rescue of me inspires me to share everything I know with you," said

Gomez. "Alas, however, those goons killed poor Eddie Anguille before he had a chance to tell me a damn thing, let alone pass me this alleged letter you seem so het up about."

Sidebar turned his head, stared at Gomez. His plaseyes glowed briefly—an intense green. "It's addressed to the Paris Police Bureau," he said as his eyes faded back to their usual silvery gray. "It says, and I quote, 'Bouchon was not one of mine. (Signed) The Unknown Soldier.'"

"Wonderful. Yes, that confirms my—"

"How'd he do that?" Scowling, Gomez touched the pocket where he'd stowed the copy of the letter.

"X-ray vision, schmuck," answered Sidebar. "It's built into all the best cameramen at Newz, Inc. And as you can see I'm one of the best."

"Bouchon was killed for some other reason, by someone else," said Natalie, hugging herself and smiling with satisfaction. "Yes, that's exactly what I figured."

"Bouchon?" said Gomez, frowning. "Oh, sí, I heard about his being knocked off."

"Don't think, please, that I don't enjoy these simple little games you're so fond of trying to play with me, Gomez, because if I'm in the right mood, they can be mildly amusing," said Natalie. "But, honestly, you better level with me from now on so that we can work side by side."

"You're absolutely right, Nat, and excuse me for not being completely open with you. I should've known I couldn't match wits with an astute reporter like you," he said apologetically. "If you could drop me near my hotel, which is the Louvre, I'll sit right down and start putting my notes in order. We'll meet for lunch *mañana* and share all."

The redhead watched his face for several silent seconds. "That would be nice, although I still don't feel you're being completely honest," she said. "You're not lying to me, are you?"

"I most certainly am not, *chiquita,*" he lied.

The door of the dining room snapped open. A lovely blonde android, clad in just about nothing, came stumbling out. There was blood splashed across her face and breasts. She bumped into Jake, caught hold of his arm, crying out, "They killed him! They murdered poor Zacky!"

Shoving the mechanical woman aside, Jake carefully crossed the threshold.

The large dining room's interior offered a simulated moonlit terrace with a long formal dining table set up on the mosaic tiles. A large rectangle had been seared out of the far wall with a disintegrator cannon and the real night showed. A chill wind was blowing into the room, carrying rain with it.

Another nearly naked female android was

still seated at the table. Most of her left side had been sliced away with a lazgun and her inner works were spilled out and dangling.

A third android, this one in the image of a naked young boy of fourteen, was leaning slackly against the stone railing of the terrace. The night rain was hitting at him and, very slowly now, he started to slide down to the tiles. When he finally landed, with a gentle thunk, his blond head separated from his torso to go rolling across the damp terrace tiles. It came to a stop against the bare leg of the female android and the bright blue eyes started blinking rapidly.

Jake had drawn his stungun from his shoulder holster. After scanning the room and determining that whoever'd broken in was long gone, he walked over to the table.

On the far side lay a slim man with wavy blond hair. They'd sliced off both his hands with a lazgun and he'd been bleeding to death. The rain was mixing with the spilled blood, thinning it and spreading it across the intricate patterns of the tiling.

Knowing it was too late to help the dying man, Jake knelt beside him. "Who did this, Rolfe?"

The IDCA agent noticed him after a few seconds. "Cardigan," he whispered.

"Who was it?"

Rolfe's bloody right arm started to rise, as though he intended to take hold of Jake's sleeve with the hand he no longer had. "Watch out . . . watch out," he said in a voice that was running down, ". . . for Excalibur."

A few choking sounds followed the last word. Then Rolfe died.

═11═

JAKE RETURNED TO the hotel suite first. Leaving most of the lights off, he went over and stood by the window. The rain had turned to mist and everything was soft and hazy out in the night.

"Maybe I've been at this business too long," he told himself. He felt tired and he had the suspicion he'd feel the same way come morning.

In the alcove the vidphone buzzed.

Jake crossed over to answer. "Yeah?"

"Hello, dear." Beth appeared on the screen, smiling.

"You called at a good time," he told her. "I was just about to start brooding."

"What I have to tell you, Jake, may not cheer you up," she said. "Perhaps you already know, but since it's being kept off the news media, perhaps you don't. I thought I'd better call you."

"What's wrong? Is your father—"

"No, it's Bennett Sands," she told him. "I just found out from Agent Griggs. Sands has disappeared from the prison near Barsetshire. They discovered he was gone roughly three hours ago."

"Damn," said Jake quietly. "How'd he escape?"

She shook her head. "No one is certain. Obviously, though, the electronic surveillance system in his room in the hospital wing had to be fooled somehow. When they made their last in-person check on Sands, he simply wasn't there. Nor anywhere else in the place."

Jake said, "That's why he was shipped over to England."

"You think so?"

"Yeah. Somebody in England has a use for Sands. And enough influence to get him transferred from NorCal," Jake said. "Plus enough connections to get him quietly sprung from a maxsec setup."

"I'm trying to find out more details," Beth said. "But ... I don't know, Jake. I keep feeling that my father knew that this was going to happen."

"Maybe he did, Beth. And I'm damn near certain Kate was expecting the escape, too."

Smiling a bit sadly, Beth said, "We don't seem to be having much luck with our relatives lately."

"Sands' daughter has dropped out of sight,

too," Jake told her. "You know that Dan's had a sort of crush on her for a long time. I'm worried he'll go hunting for her and get himself tangled up with Sands and the people who sprung him."

"Dan's inherited your smartness. He won't do anything dumb," she assured him. "By the way, on an entirely different topic—I miss you."

"I have similar feelings about you."

"Any idea how soon you'll be home?"

"Not yet, and after we finish up here in Paris I want to go over to England to see Dan."

"And Kate?"

"Not Kate, no." They watched each other for a moment on the vidphone.

"Well, when you get to London, I have a couple of people you might want to look up. In case you happen to need assistance in certain areas," Beth said. "There's Marj Lofton, an old friend of mine. She used to be a very successful Associate Professor of Robotics at SoCal Tech. Three years ago, though, Marj decided she wanted to help people more directly and she went home to England to get involved in social work. She knows a lot about London lowlife."

"Yeah, I may need her."

"And my other friend, Denis Gilford, is now a reporter for *The London FaxTimes*. He always has access to all sorts of information nobody is supposed to have."

"Another one of your former suitors?"

"Denis is a friend, that's all."

"Okay, I'll add him to my list of things to see in London." He smiled.

"I think you'll enjoy him. Well, I have to go now. Remember, I love you, Jake."

Jake said, "And I love you."

The screen went blank.

He was alive again.

Sitting there, breathing in and out regularly, none of the other passengers paying him any mind.

Just a sad-looking young man, far as they could tell, bundled up in a large black overcoat with a knit cap pulled down low on his head. Sitting there, breathing in and out regularly. Nobody, not one of the damn idiots sharing this car in the London Underground Tubetrain, was aware of who he was.

He was death.

Not for them, not tonight anyway. But you never could tell. Maybe some night, maybe one of them would have to die.

He never knew. He'd simply be alive again, breathing in and out regularly, and a name would be given to him. Tonight was an easy one, without a lot of travel involved.

Tonight he just had to kill someone close to home.

Not that he minded traveling. Not that he liked traveling either. The part he didn't much care for, although he hadn't complained yet, was memorizing all the details about the person he had to kill.

That meant studying, which was too much like school. After all, he'd been out of college for . . . Well, he didn't have a complete memory about that. It had been a while ago anyway.

The voxbox in the ceiling of the car announced, "Coming into Paddington Station."

The young man waited until a few other passengers had gotten up to move toward the doors. Then he stood.

The underground train silently halted, the doors silently drifted open.

As he went out the door onto the platform, the right-hand pocket of his black overcoat banged against the frame and produced a metallic crack. But nobody noticed.

The young man walked toward an exit, not hurrying, breathing in and out regularly. The weapons detector in the gate didn't make a sound as he passed through. It was a simple-minded mechanism, incapable of getting around the antidetection gadget he carried in his pocket along with his stungun and his lazgun.

He got on a motoramp and let it carry him up to the street. He made his way over to Level One of Praed Street, not bothered by the thick, chill fog that choked the late night thoroughfare.

Thoroughfare. That was a nice word. It showed that he had a large and useful vocabulary. He sometimes, however, wished that his memory matched his vocabulary.

On his left the words TOURIST PUB floated, glowing a prickly red, in the fog. The young man continued on until he reached Level One of the Edgware Road. He halted for a moment, listening, glancing casually around him.

Nobody was following him, no one was paying him undue attention. It was safe to go ahead with tonight's killing.

Nodding, he climbed the ramp to Level 2 of Edgware. He patted the other pocket of his overcoat. It contained, neatly folded, the note he had to leave on the corpse after he cut it into four.

—= 12 =—

As soon as the room service robot took its leave, Gomez carried his bottle of ale over to a soft armchair. "What do you figure we have, Jake?" he asked as he sat down. "A lot of pieces of one big jigsaw puzzle or a few pieces for several little puzzles?"

"I'm not sure yet." Jake was leaning against the wall near the window, arms folded, looking out at the night city. "My bet right now is that most of this does tie together."

"Which means the Teklords are behind it all." He drank directly from the chilled bottle.

"They didn't, I don't think, break Sands out of prison just because they like him or because they owe the guy a favor. My feeling is there's some big plan in the works and they need him for that."

Gomez studied the ceiling. "It's possible, *amigo*, that Bouchon found out something about that same plan and was bumped off to hush him up."

Jake crossed over to pick up the copy of the Unknown Soldier letter from atop the coffee table. "If this is real, it definitely establishes that he wasn't killed by our serial killer." He absently folded the note. "Zack Rolfe knew something, too. My guess is he helped set up Bouchon."

"You say Madame Nana, AKA our old chum Lulu Blueberry, claims to know absolutely *nada?*"

"We had a lively chat after I left the private dining room and while we were waiting for the Paris cops to get there. She claims she wasn't stalling me, didn't tip anyone that I'd come looking for Rolfe, didn't know anyone was planning to drop in at her establishment to kill the guy. Furthermore, the word Excalibur means nothing at all to Lulu."

"I'll get somebody digging deep into her recent activities and associations," promised his partner. "As to Excalibur . . ."

"Yeah?"

"A very dim chime went off deep in my *cabeza* when first you mentioned it." Gomez shook his head. "Nope, I am still unable to dredge anything up."

Tossing the folded note back on the table, Jake wandered again to the window. "Sands knows quite a lot about Professor Kittridge's anti-Tek system," he said. "He might also know how to sabotage it."

"Could be that *hombre* also can tell certain selected Tek potentates how to render themselves immune to the upcoming anti-Tek passover that Kittridge and the IDCA are planning," speculated Gomez. "If a few dealers retained a supply of usable Tek chips, after most of the chips have been turned flooey, then they'd have a very lucrative monopoly."

"Tomorrow we'll also find out more about the life and times of Zack Rolfe," said Jake. "And we have to find out what he meant by Excalibur."

After taking another swig, Gomez again contemplated the ceiling. "Is it worth the anguish?" he murmured.

"Is what?"

"I was carrying on a debate with myself," confessed his partner. "It's possible that I can sweet-talk a stewpot of useful info out of the fair Natalie. I'm just not sure if I want to get snared in her web yet again."

"Natalie can be a pest, but you've worked with her before," Jake pointed out. "And she has been moderately helpful, which she was over in Japan a few months back. And just because she's fond of you, Sid, that doesn't mean her judgment is flawed in other areas."

Gomez arose, smiling. "Come to think of it, *amigo,* the fact that she admires me does indicate a certain smartness on her part, doesn't

it?" he said. "I guess I'll keep that lunch date."
His eyes twinkled.

The young man in the black overcoat slowed
his pace. A half block ahead of him on his
right, only partially visible in the night fog,
rose the three tall towers of the Maida Vale
Complex. Jonathan Ainsworth, member of the
British Senate, was on the 18th floor of Tower
2 just now.

He was visiting, unbeknownst to his wife, a
young woman named Felicity Blore.

Silly name.

Silly young woman, for that matter.

The young man, breathing in and out regularly, walked on by the apartment towers.

Just beyond them was Visitors' Landing
Area 2. There were approximately sixty skycars and skyvans parked there, swathed in fog.
The globe lights ringing the wide area were all
blurred by the thick mist.

The young man walked up to the small plastiglass guard hut. Wiping at his nose with the
back of his left hand, he asked, in a voice not
his own, "Can I maybe, gov, earn a bit of lolly
by polishing up some of them cars?"

The guardbot was large and gray. He came
lumbering out of the hut to eye the young man.

"I'm 'avin' 'ard times, I am," the young man
continued. "Why, I ain't eaten since—"

"Go away." The robot had a deep, rumbling
voice.

"Aw, I bet a lot of these toffs wouldn't mind me earnin' a—"

"Go away, young fellow me lad, or I shall have the law on you."

Lurching, the young man put his hand on the guardbot's shoulder to keep his balance. That contact produced a faint, unexpected buzzing sound.

The robot suddenly stiffened, metallic eyelids clicking rapidly for nearly half a minute.

"Back into your shed," ordered the young man. "I have a permit to visit here and you've seen it."

"Yes, sir. Right you are, sir." Bowing once, the robot withdrew to his dim-lit hut.

The young man crossed over into the lot and walked straight to an expensive crimson skycar parked in the third row.

A uniformed human pilot, a thickset man of thirty, was dozing in the driveseat.

After easing his stungun out with his right hand, the young man held it down at his side. With his left he tapped nervously on the window.

The pilot jerked awake, blinking. "What the devil you want?" he asked, lowering his window a few inches.

"Oh, dear, I do hope you're the person I'm seeking, sir. This is just awful."

"What the devil are you nattering about?"

"Are you Simmons? Bert Simmons?"

"I am. What's it to you?"

"Well, you see, I'm Alfred Swindon and I'm employed over there in Tower 2," he explained excitedly. "I very much fear that your employer—if your employer is Senator Ainsworth—is he?"

"Yes, now quit your acting daft and explain yourself."

"He's had—it's Senator Ainsworth I'm alluding to—he's suffered some sort of seizure. In Miss Blore's apartment unfortunately. I thought perhaps under the circumstances that you might wish to remove him to a more—"

"All right, twit." The door came popping open and the thickset man stepped out. "I'll come up there with you, see, and take charge."

"Yes, you strike me as the sort of gentleman who can handle these embarrassing situations." The young man shot the pilot with his stungun.

Then he hopped deftly backward, out of the way of the falling man.

After a careful look around, he stored the unconscious man in the back compartment of the skycar.

Next he took off his cap and removed his overcoat.

He was ready.

He was wearing a tattered, bloodstained uniform. It was the kind worn by the United Nations Combat Forces during the Brazil Wars years ago. His hair was cut short, his moustache was bushy, and from his left ear dangled an earring made of a Brazilian coin.

It was important that Senator Ainsworth see him in this uniform in the last minutes of his life. Ainsworth had been an enthusiastic supporter of those wars. He'd spearheaded the reinstatement of the draft in Great Britain. A lot of young men had died because of him.

The young man took his other gun out of his pocket. He removed the note and tucked it into the breast pocket of his tunic.

After folding up the coat and placing it carefully on the passenger seat, he slid in and sat where the pilot had been.

He didn't mind waiting.

≡ 13 ≡

THE COPPER-PLATED robot chef set their breakfast plates before them. "Allow me to apologize
again, messieurs," he said, fluffing his crisp
white chef's hat. "In all my years at the Louvre
Hotel, I assure you, the waiter androids have
never before gone out on strike. Machines that
put on airs . . . Bah!" Turning briskly, he went
striding away across the large, vaulted dining
room.

Gomez picked up his knife and fork. "I've
been meditating about Excalibur," he said,
gesturing with his knife. "It was King Arthur's
sword, *sí?*"

After sampling his soycaf, Jake said, "According to legend, yes."

"My informative buddy, Limehouse, is what
you might call an Anglophile. A monarchist
actually, who yearns to see a king back in
place," continued his partner. "The gent has

107

his underground digs lavishly plastered with pics of British royalty."

"And?"

"Yesterday, amongst the newer portraits, I glimpsed one of a chinless chap called King Arthur II."

"When did he reign?"

"He hasn't, *amigo*. Not yet, though he's apparently standing by." Gomez used his knife and fork on his fakbacon. "Should the present English system, with prez, vice prez and so on, collapse or be overthrown, then Artie would dig up the discarded throne, dust it off, and hop aboard. He'd rule as King Art II."

"Wonder how many supporters he has."

"Quien sabe? But I'll find out," he promised. "It could be there's an Excalibur associated with this guy."

"Sands is in England, so is this Arthur Number 2, so it—"

"A thousand pardons, Monsieur Cardigan." It was the coppery chef again, cap in hand. "There's an important phonemessage for you."

"Can I take it in the lobby?"

"Oui, in Alcove 6." He glanced down at Gomez's plate. "What's wrong with the crêpes?"

"Not a blessed thing."

"I notice you're toying with them and not eating them."

"That's my breakfast style. Don't take it as a critique."

"As you say." Replacing his snowy white cap atop his copper-plated head, he walked away.

"Keep toying," said Jake, leaving the table. "I'll be back soon."

Jake's former wife frowned at him from the phonescreen. "Do you know where he is?" Her voice was touched with anger.

"Sands? Nope, I don't, but—"

"What in the hell are you talking about, Jake?"

"Bennett Sands. He disappeared from prison late last night."

She inhaled sharply. "That's impossible. Nobody can get out of a place like that."

"With the right sort of help you can get out of anywhere," he told her. "Didn't you know Sands was planning to escape?"

"No, of course not. Simply because I once worked for him, that doesn't mean I'm involved with what he does now," she said. "But that's not why I called you."

"Is it Dan?"

"Yes. They called me just now to say Danny's run away from the Bunter Academy." She started to cry softly. "Sometime last night, they think, Jake. I really am trying to be a good mother . . . But Danny . . . ever since you got out of prison . . . I don't know, he hasn't been happy and there's been trouble at every school he—"

"What about Nancy Sands? Has she turned up?"

"No, she hasn't. That hadn't occurred to me . . . Do you think she and Danny might be together?"

"Kate, I don't really give a damn how closely you're tied up with Sands." He leaned closer to the screen. "But if you know where he's holed up, tell me. His daughter's probably with him by now, and if Dan knows where she's gone, he may try to join her."

"For God's sake, I'm not Bennett's mistress—or his accomplice," she shouted at him. "Danny's my son, too, remember? Do you really think I'd let him get involved with something like this?"

"You don't know where Sands is?"

"No, damn it, no! I just want to find my son," she said, sobbing. "I contacted you because I thought you could help. But if all you're going to do is criticize me and preach, I'm hanging up."

"Okay, okay," he interrupted. "I'll come over to England, be there in a few hours. I'll find Dan."

"Can you come here first? I—"

"I won't have time," he told her. "But I'll keep in touch with you by phone. I'll let you know whatever I find out."

She asked him, "You're never going to forgive me for divorcing you while you were in prison, are you?"

"Probably not." He hung up.

Jake's first-class compartment on the Paris-London subtrain was mildly annoyed with him. "But, really, sir," it was saying out of the voxbox implanted just below the phonescreen, "the complete luncheon is included in the price of your ticket, don't you see? If you hadn't wished to partake of the luncheon, why, may I ask, did you book first class?"

"For privacy," explained Jake. "Now, please, shut yourself off."

The voxbox went dead.

Jake moved across the small, blankwalled compartment and activated the vidphone. He punched out a London number.

Thirty seconds later a ballheaded gray robot appeared on the screen. "Hewitt Inquiry Agency here."

"Jake Cardigan for Arthur Bairnhouse."

"Ah, yes, Mr. Cardigan. A moment, if you will."

Bairnhouse was a pink-faced, moderately overweight man of forty, dressed in a tweedy fashion. His office, what could be seen of it on the phonescreen, was paneled in dark real wood. "Glad you've called, Cardigan," he said.

"Anything on Dan yet?"

"Nothing thus far, I'm afraid," replied the

detective. "We do, however, have something fairly definite on the Sands girl."

"It's my hunch she's going to join her father."

"It doesn't, actually, look as though that's the situation." Bairnhouse rubbed at his broad flat nose with his thumb. "We have reason to believe that she's gone into a very rough, crime-infested section of London. An area dominated by youth gangs and not, I'd venture to say, a likely area for a man like Bennett Sands to go to ground."

"Dan is probably following her. He may even have heard from Nancy and know where she is."

"When we had our violent revolution some sixty years ago, Cardigan, a great deal of damage was done to large sections of London. The area around Buckingham Palace was especially hard hit," the plump detective told him. "For various reasons, some of them symbolic, a goodly portion of that damage was never remedied. Now the children control the area and it is, to state the case quite simply, not a safe place for a decent young person to be roaming unprotected."

"Soon as I reach London, I'll have to head for there to start hunting for my son."

"Drop by our offices first, will you, Cardigan? We should have more information by the time you arrive, and I can be of some help in preparing you for the pitfalls," said the detective. "There will be, believe me, a great many pitfalls."

"Yeah, I'm expecting that," said Jake.

—=14=—

THE PREVIOUS EVENING, all across Barsetshire,
it had been snowing. A quiet, gentle snow that
fell straight down through the dark sky. From
the side door of Dan's dorm building to the
stone wall that surrounded the grounds of
Bunter Academy was roughly two hundred
yards. Dan had stood in the doorway for nearly
ten minutes, waiting and listening. The snow
kept flickering silently down. Far off, probably
at the estate up on the hill, a lone dog barked
once.

Readjusting the tan neowool muffler that
Nancy Sands had given him just two weeks
ago, Dan went darting out into the open. He
ran across the white ground, snow quietly
crackling underfoot. When he reached the six-
foot-high wall, he struggled up it and grasped
the top with both hands. Breathing hard, Dan
pulled himself up and stretched out flat for a
moment.

The five gray buildings that made up the school looked flat and two-dimensional through the soft, fluttering snow. No one seemed to have noticed him. Dan took a deep breath before dropping off the wall to the muffled turf on the other side.

Getting to his feet, he brushed snow off his dark jacket and trousers. He started walking rapidly along the road that led to the village. It was two miles distant, but Dan figured he could make it there in under half an hour.

He glanced back over his shoulder a few times. As soon as he was sure no one from the academy had been aware of his unauthorized departure or had come after him, he quit looking back.

And so he never saw the dark figure that moved out of the stand of trees and started to tail him.

Night was well along by the time Dan reached the center of the village. The windows of the one- and two-story metal and plastiglass shops glowed pale yellow, and a light wind was swirling the snowflakes as they fell.

Hurrying, Dan turned onto a narrow street marked Antiquity Lane. All the shops and restaurants here had been designed to resemble nineteenth-century structures. There were tiled roofs, thatched roofs, timbered fronts, oaken shutters, stained glass windows. An android beggar boy, dressed in raggedy mismatched nineteenth-century clothes, stood shivering in front of Dan's destination.

"Spare me tuppence, sir?"

Ignoring him, Dan entered the Maze Tea Shop. There seemed to be a fire blazing briskly in the deep stone fireplace of the simulated parlor.

A plump maternal android in appropriate dress came bustling over, smiling broadly, wiping her hands on her large white apron. "How may I serve you, young master?"

He said, "I'm supposed to meet someone here."

"Bless me if I don't sense another romance in the making," said the proprietress, chuckling. "Would it be a pretty, dark-haired young lady that you're seeking?"

"Yes, it is."

"She's here already, anxiously awaiting you. You'll find the dear thing out in the maze and looking pretty as a picture." The android pointed toward a doorway on the left. "Follow the arrow, mind."

Dan went through the doorway and found himself in what looked to be a vast stretch of outdoor garden. A maze made of high thick hedges filled most of the grounds.

"Arrow," reminded the proprietress from the parlor.

On the grassy path at his feet a yard-long arrow of red light appeared. The arrow started moving slowly forward.

Following, Dan was led along pathways and through the green, leafy corridors of the hologram maze. When the arrow reached a small, sunlit clearing, it faded away.

Seated alone at a round white wicker table was a slim young woman of sixteen. Her hair was dark and long and she had on the uniform of a nearby school. "I thought perhaps they wouldn't give you permission to leave the academy this late in the evening," she said.

"They didn't." He sat opposite her.

"Are you likely to get in trouble, Daniel?"

"I am, yeah," he admitted. "You said on the phone that you had something new to tell me about Nancy, Jillian."

"I think perhaps I do."

"Perhaps?"

Jillian Kearny asked him, "Would you care for some tea, Daniel?"

"Not especially. Do you know where she is?"

"I have a notion," the girl answered. "I was considering telling the McCays, the people she's been staying with, yet I suspect Nancy didn't trust them too awfully much."

"Are they involved in this?"

"I'm not certain." Carefully Jillian poured herself a cup from the china teapot. "I've only known Nancy, keep in mind, a few weeks," she reminded him. "In that time, however, we have become rather close friends."

"I know. That's why when you phoned—"

"I've been going over all this in my head ever since Nancy ran away."

"You're sure she did run away on her own, that she wasn't taken?"

"Yes, I am. A few days, you see, before she left the McCays I think something unpleasant happened there."

"Did they hurt her?"

"Nothing of that sort, Daniel. Nancy did, though, discover something that upset her a great deal. I was aware that she was upset, but she wouldn't confide any details."

"She didn't even hint at what she'd found out?"

"She simply didn't wish to talk about what was bothering her." Jillian paused, sipped her tea. "My impression is that this had something to do with her father."

"Did she mention him?"

"Rather she stopped talking about him. Which is the point, do you see? Up until then she'd mentioned Mr. Sands quite often," said the girl. "Nancy always spoke of him in a positive way, defending his reputation. She firmly believed, I'm convinced, that he was innocent of all he'd been charged with and was unjustly serving time in prison."

"But then she must have found out something negative about Bennett?"

"Yes. Though I am of course merely guessing."

"Why did she go away?"

119

"She did say that she wanted very much to get away by herself for a while, away from under the eyes of the McCays. Nancy felt she needed time to work things out. I had the impression she wasn't certain what to do about whatever it was that she'd learned."

Dan rested both elbows on the tabletop. "Okay, but when I talked to you before, Jill, you told me you had no idea where she might've gone," he said. "But now you do?"

"I've been turning things over in my mind, trying to come up with some memory that might help." She leaned forward. "Just today I recalled that Nancy told me—oh, quite soon after we'd met at school—that a friend of hers, an American girl whom she'd known at home, had been living in England. This friend had decided to run away and was hiding out in one of the wilder sections of London."

"Did Nancy tell you who this girl was and where she was living?"

"Yes, since the friend had apparently communicated with her once or twice. It's a section of London that's ruled by street gangs."

"Can you tell me where to find the girl?"

Nodding, Jillian took a slip of paper from her tunic pocket. "I've written down all that I remembered, Daniel," she said slowly. "I find, I'm afraid, that I'm simply not brave enough to go to the authorities directly with this. Since you're a close friend of Nancy's with a father who's a detective, perhaps you can see that this information gets to the proper people. It may not be worth anything, but I felt I must confide in someone."

"I'll handle it." Dan reached across to take the slip of paper from her.

"Nancy has very romantic and naive notions about what life is like in that part of London," Jillian said. "If she thinks of it as a refuge for confused young women, she's in for a rude awakening. The kid gangs that—" She paused, looking into his face, and frowning. "Surely, Daniel, you're not thinking of going in there after her yourself?"

He rose up. "Thanks for passing this information along, Jill," he said. "I'll be in touch."

"It's really too dangerous. You simply can't go there."

"Yes, I can," he said and left.

≡ 15 ≡

THE SCOTLAND YARD robots were extremely polite to Jake.

There were two of them, big gunmetal bots wearing plaid overcoats and bowler hats. When Jake hit the platform at the London subtrain station, they were waiting close to the spot where his compartment had come to a stop.

Tipping their hats in unison, they both stepped into his path. "Mr. Cardigan, isn't it?" inquired the one on the left.

"Yeah, it is."

They both pointed to their metallic foreheads. Small plates in each skull slid silently aside to reveal tiny viewscreens. On each appeared authenticated copies of their police credentials. After allowing sufficient time for Jake to read the material, the panels snapped shut.

"We trust, sir, that you enjoyed a pleasant journey from the continent?" inquired the one on the right.

"Trip wasn't bad," admitted Jake. "And I appreciate Scotland Yard's sending you down to inquire. Now I'll bid you farewell."

"If you wouldn't mind, Mr. Cardigan," requested the one on the left in deferential tones, "we'd be most gratified were you to accompany us."

"Haven't got the time, fellas."

The one on the right said, "Perhaps if we were to explain the current statutes applying to formal requests for an interview, sir?"

"Yes, that might be a jolly good idea," seconded the one on the left.

"I know," cut in Jake. "You have the right to use a stungun on me if I don't come along willingly. That's a dimwit law, by the way."

"Ah, but then, sir, we merely carry out the laws as they are written." The robot on the right adjusted his bowler hat on his round metal head. "You are not, please understand, being arrested, nor are we implying in any manner or form that you might perhaps be a wrongdoer."

"Not at all. We are simply inviting you to step around to the Yard, Mr. Cardigan."

"To see who?"

"Our Inspector Beckford."

"Beckford," said Jake with a definite lack of respect.

"You're acquainted with the inspector, I believe."

"I know Becky," admitted Jake. "He is, to use a technical term, a first-class jerk. Really, fellas, there's absolutely no good reason why—"

"Since you're familiar not only with Inspector Beckford, but with British law in all its richness and complexity, Mr. Cardigan," said the robot on the right, "you must be aware that if you dawdle and stall much longer, we'll be compelled to stun you and transport you to the Yard in a medivan."

"Right, sure," said Jake. "Okay, I may as well go there conscious."

"Come along this way, sir." The one on the left got a firm grip on Jake's arm.

"We appreciate your spirit of cooperation, sir." The one on the right took hold of Jake's other arm. "Off we go to Scotland Yard."

Gomez was lying again.

He was doing it while guiding his rented landcar through the crowded lower-level streets of Paris, glancing now and then at the vidscreen implanted in the dash.

An angry Natalie Dent was glaring at him on the screen. "But you weren't at your darn hotel or anywhere in the vicinity," she said accusingly. "It seems to me that when you make a date to meet someone for lunch, Gomez, you either ought to show up at the preordained spot or make other arrangements."

"Chiquita, I left a message for you at the desk."

"There wasn't anybody at the desk except some nitwit robot chef who claimed he was filling in because the clerks were off taking a strike vote."

"Nat, had not a sudden important situation come up, we'd be lunching right this minute in some ritz bistro and exchanging important info."

"Where are you?" the red-haired reporter asked pointedly.

"En route to the American Embassy," he assured her. "It's a routine check of my travel papers."

"That doesn't, if you'll pardon my mentioning it, sound like anything very serious to me, Gomez."

"Not to you, not to me, *sí,* but to the embassy it is."

"It seems to me that a man with your gall could simply have told them you had a lunch date."

"It isn't Cosmos policy to ignore official requests like this." Gomez turned his car onto a quirky lane. "Ah, but I see the embassy looming up ahead, so I must bid you a reluctant *adiós.*"

"What I'm seeing—and granted I'm only getting a somewhat cockeyed view of what the phonecam is seeing over your droopy shoulder and out the dingy back window of that clunky vehicle you're joyriding around in, but what I'm seeing looks an awful lot like the neighborhood down along the Seine. Where your present client happens to live The embassy, on the other hand, is way over on—"

"Es verdad," admitted the detective as he drove into a parking area. "But actually I'm meeting the ambassador himself down here. Don't know why I said embassy, I meant I saw the ambassador looming up. It's his custom, *pobrecita,* to take a stroll along the river after lunch."

"How can you handle paperwork while strolling along the river?"

"I asked him the very same question, Nat, and he replied, 'You simply have to trust your government, Mr. Gomez.' I must rush off now."

"I'm not the sort of person who likes to issue dire warnings," said Natalie on the phonescreen. "But, Gomez, you darn well better get together with me before the sun sets on another day and be prepared to share some facts about the Bouchon killing with me. Otherwise my seldom-seen vindictive side will work out some very unpleasant consequences."

"We'll meet later in the day," he promised, unbuckling his safety gear.

"Where? When?"

"Ah, those are excellent reporter questions, Nat. I'll phone and set up a meeting," he said.

"Adiós." He clicked off the phone, dived out of the car.

Their client had contacted him a half hour earlier and told him it was important that she see him at once. That was—well, it was one of the reasons anyway—why Gomez had ditched Natalie Dent.

He went hurrying out of the parking area, slowing only to grab the chit that came out of the slot in the chest of the mechanical attendant.

When he got to the gangway leading up to Madeleine Bouchon's houseboat, there was no sign of the chrome-plated guardbot. Not even his wrought-iron chair was there. Poking his tongue into his cheek, Gomez scanned the area along the river. A few plump pigeons were strutting on the imitation cobblestones. An android was sitting under a tree playing the accordion.

Uneasy, but unable to pinpoint anything else out of the ordinary beyond the absence of the guard, Gomez started slowly up the gangway. Less than halfway to the deck he noticed a beret floating down in the water. It looked a lot like the one the robot had tipped to them on their last visit.

He took a few more steps toward the boat, then noticed the wrought-iron chair underwater down in the river, its legs sticking up.

From the conservatory on the houseboat came the sudden cry of a woman in pain.

═16═

THERE WAS NOTHING in Inspector Beckford's large off-white office except the inspector, two off-white chairs, and Jake.

After dusting off the seat of his chair with a plyochief, the trim blond Beckford seated himself. "My associates tell me you alluded to me as a first-class jerk," he said.

"I didn't want to use stronger language in front of them," said Jake. "I never like to see a robot blush. What exactly do you want?"

"They also stated that you referred to me as Becky."

"Not a term of endearment." Jake spun the chair around, sat straddling it.

"I prefer not to be called Becky, Cardigan."

"Fine. Why am I here?"

"That's precisely what I'm most anxious to learn," Inspector Beckford told him. "What does bring you to London?"

"Personal business."

"You may recall that I didn't care for you when you were a California police officer and came poking around in London some years ago," said the inspector. "I find I care for you even less now that you're nothing more than a private investigator."

Jake reflected. "I guess I dislike you about the same as I did back seven years ago. No more, no less."

Beckford rested his hands on his knees, watching Jake. "This Unknown Soldier case is one I don't want anyone interfering with," he warned.

"Whoa now. You don't have any jurisdiction in France."

"Don't try playing schoolboy games with me. You're much too along in years to bring it off, Cardigan."

Grinning, Jake asked, "There's been a new killing, huh? Right here in England."

"I assumed you already knew that. Isn't that why you came over to England in such a rush?"

"No, it isn't. Who's the victim?"

"Senator Ainsworth. He was murdered outside the apartment of his current mistress," answered the inspector. "His skycar pilot was only stunned. Ainsworth, of course, was killed by having his body quartered."

"Do all the details match the other killings?"

Leaving his chair, Beckford slowly walked to the room's solitary window. He stared out at the gray day. "The description of the killer matches, his method was the same."

"But something's bothering you?"

"I know you've been hired to look into the murder of Joseph Bouchon. Are there really any indications that he wasn't a victim of the Unknown Soldier?"

"Some, yeah."

The inspector returned to his chair. He dusted it again before reseating himself. "The note he left last night contained a variation."

"Which was?"

"In addition to his usual message, he added a postscript. It consisted of one word— 'True.'"

"Which could mean," said Jake, "that this was a true Unknown Soldier kill and not an imitation."

"You're thoroughly convinced, are you, that there are two separate killers?"

"There seem to be," said Jake. "There's the Unknown Soldier and there's the copycat who did in Bouchon."

Inspector Beckford said, "You give me your word that you aren't in England to interfere in my investigation?"

"Until you told me, I didn't even know there'd been a new killing."

"Where are you staying?"

"The Crystal Palace Hotel."

The inspector stood. "You may consider our interview at an end."

* * *

Gomez recognized both of the goons who were standing in the conservatory, glaring down at the sprawled Madeleine Bouchon. They were the exact same lads who'd burst into Eddie Anguille's room at the Hotel Algiers yesterday. In fact, the needlegun thrust in the belt of the larger of the two louts was probably the same one that had been used to shred the informer to tatters.

"What I really need right now," the lurking detective said to himself, "is a diversion."

He was crouched in the galley next to the conservatory, having snuck about the houseboat and slipped in there. He was watching the two husky men threaten Madeleine, his eye to the slit of the barely open door between the two rooms.

"You understand?" The one with the needlegun squatted next to the woman. "You better forget all about your husband's murder, lady."

His companion squatted, too, grabbing hold of her blonde hair. He yanked hard, jerking her head up clear of the carpeting. "All you got to remember is that the Unknown Soldier killed the bastard."

Gomez overcame an impulse to go charging in there. He looked around and noticed Maurice, the serving robot, standing stiff in a shadowy corner of the galley. Quickly, quietly, he slid over to the robot and activated it.

"Oui? How may I be of—"

"Quiet, please," urged the detective in a whisper. "What I want you to do, Maurice, is walk right into the conservatory and pretend those two lunks in there ordered drinks. Beer, I think, will be the best."

"Monsieur, I fear I don't exactly comprehend—"

"Just listen. You miss the glass and, making it look like an accident, you spritz beer into one of the guys' faces. Then, acting flustered, you drop the glass on his foot. Do you think you can play a scene like that, Maurice old chum, without—"

"One hates to perform one's duties in such a slovenly fashion."

"Mrs. Bouchon is in danger. But you and I working as a team can save her."

"Ah . . . but in that case I am yours to command." The robot rolled to the door, pushed it open, and went into the next room.

"Hey—who the hell are you?"

"Here is your beer, monsieur."

"Aw, this ain't the time for booze or . . . Yikes!"

"Watch out, you stupid tincan, you shot it in his kisser and . . . Ow! Don't roll over my damn foot."

Gomez entered then, stungun in hand.

He fired at the one with the needlegun.

The other lout was wiping beer off his face with a plyochief.

The other one had reached for the needlegun, but the stungun beam had hit him square in the chest before his fingers closed on the butt. He stiffened, executed a jerky shuffle off to his left, stumbled, went crashing into the glasswall of the big room.

The remaining goon noticed Gomez, through beer-blurred eyes, and grabbed for his lazgun.

"Nope." Gomez shot him.

When the sizzling beam hit this one, he went swooping backwards. He flapped his arms for a moment, as though he had suddenly decided he knew how to fly. But he never got airborne. Instead he fell over with an impressive thud, bounced once, and lay still.

Tucking away his stungun, Gomez ran to Madeleine's side, saying to the robot in passing, "You did a dandy job of distracting them, Maurice."

"It was rather effective, *oui.*"

Kneeling, Gomez slid an arm around the blonde woman's slim shoulders. "You all right, ma'am?"

"I'm not too bad. They've only been here a few moments."

He helped her to stand. "From what I overheard, they'd like you to stop looking into your husband's death."

"We'll keep on," she said. "In fact, we have something important to take care of as soon as we can."

—≡ 17 ≡—

SHOWERED AND CHANGED, Jake stepped back into the living room of his hotel suite.

There was a lean, pale man sitting relaxedly up on his bed, smoking a potcig and casually rummaging through the contents of his suitcase. "These aren't from the best shops, old man," he observed, tossing two of Jake's tunics back into the case. "But then, one supposes, even the best shops in Greater Los Angeles aren't exactly what one would dub *haute mode*."

"Lucky for you my stungun is sitting way over there on that table. Who are you?"

"It's a wonder, you know, that you can still even fit yourself into some of these togs," continued the lean, pale man. "You're getting a trifle thick in the middle. I can't, for the life of me, understand how Beth could describe you as—"

"Are you, possibly, Denis Gilford?"

"Certainly." Gilford took a long, relaxed drag of his potcig. "One assumed you'd recognize one. My portrait, after all, does appear daily over my highly respected column in the *FaxTimes.*"

"Who let you in here?"

"Ah, I happen to be something of an amateur cracksman." Flipping Jake's suitcase shut, the reporter shoved it farther across the bed. "Having a gift for breaking and entering can aid one in one's journalistic career."

"Tell you what," said Jake. "This meeting got going a little too informally for me. Suppose you get out of here now. If I decide I need your help, I'll contact you."

"I know that you spun Beth a yarn about coming to London solely to seek your wayward offspring." Gilford swung his legs over the edge of the bed. "It's my feeling, and one that old Becky of Scotland Yard apparently shares, that you're really in Blighty to track down the Unknown Soldier."

Crossing to the table, Jake picked up his stungun and shoulder holster and strapped it on. "Nice to have met you."

"Allow one to give you a bit of advice, old man. It would be much safer were you to allow old U.S. to go about his slaughtering."

"Oh, so?"

"Besides which, most of the rascals he's rid

the world of so far richly deserved being chopped up."

"You serve in either of the Brazil Wars?"

"One was a dashing frontline correspondent in the final go-round," answered Gilford, standing up and stretching. "I ran into a great many oafs back then who were ripe for quartering. One sometimes wonders why our Unknown Soldier has waited so long to pay them off."

Jake opened the door. "Goodbye now."

"I did inform Beth, when the dear girl buzzed me earlier, that I strongly doubted that you were the sort of fellow I'd hit it off with."

"There's another example of your astuteness, Gilford."

"However, Cardigan, old man, if you actually are seeking a lost child and need any information, do get in touch." Smiling lazily, he strolled past Jake and into the corridor.

As they drove along the Champs-Élysées, which was part real and part simulation, Gomez asked Madeleine more about the young man they were en route to visit.

She said, "I don't know Michel Chasseriau at all well. Even though he was associated with my husband at the International Drug Control Agency, I was quite surprised when he phoned me this morning."

"You've met the lad before?"

"Yes, once or twice."

"So you're not exactly an expert on his character? He could be conning you, maybe even setting you up for another encounter with goons."

"That's possible, yes, which is why I want you along," she answered. "You'll want to turn right up ahead, Mr. Gomez, and get onto the Avenue de Friedland."

"Let's go over again what he told you over the phone." Gomez made the indicated turn.

"Chasseriau seemed sincere—sincere and extremely nervous. He's young, not more than twenty-five, and he strikes me as rather a timid person," said the widow. "He's been away from the office since Joseph's death, with the excuse that he was ill. He told me, however, that he'd been staying home so that he could do a great deal of soul-searching."

"*Sí.* I used to do a lot of that when I was in my twenties."

"He claims to know something important about my husband's death. He's made up his mind he must tell me."

"But he didn't supply any details over the phone?"

"He was vague. He insisted he wanted to tell me in person."

"He must've sounded convincing."

"He did," she said. "You want to turn onto this side street ahead, then park."

Gomez did that.

The young IDCA agent had a flat on the third floor of a narrow brix building.

"What sort of music would you like to hear, madame and monsieur?" inquired the elevator.

"Let's try silence, *por favor*."

"As you wish," said the voxbox in the dark neowood ceiling of the rising cage.

When Gomez saw that the door of Chasseriau's flat was a few inches ajar, he caught Madeleine's arm. "Wait here," he cautioned.

He pressed himself to the plaswall next to the opening, listening as he slipped his stungun out. Nothing but the routine hums and murmurs of the flat reached his ears.

Nodding once, he reached out and shoved the door open wide.

Nothing happened.

After counting to thirty, in Spanish, he risked a look inside the quiet flat.

There was no one in the small living room. On a plastiglass bench sat an open suitcase with some clothes wadded into it.

Gomez let out his breath, went walking in. The flat consisted of the small living room, a small bedroom, a small bathroom, and a tiny servokitchen. There was no sign of the young IDCA agent in any of them, but it looked to the detective as though Chasseriau had done some hasty packing and departed. Left in such haste that he'd neglected to take along the suitcase that was still sitting in the living room.

Gomez went over toward the door of the flat

to communicate his findings to Madeleine. As he neared the open doorway, he heard voices in conversation.

Stungun ready, he dived into the hall.

"I was just explaining to Mrs. Bouchon, Gomez, that even though you've broken yet another vow and continue to ditch me, which is something I'd really take to heart were it not for the fact that I have a very positive image of myself, I'm still willing to play ball with you," said Natalie Dent, eyeing him in a not completely cordial manner. "By the way, the fact that I'm here should indicate, even to someone as peabrained as you sometimes appear to be, that my sources are as good as yours. If not actually better."

Madeleine asked him, "You do know this young lady?"

"We're longtime pals." Gomez put his stungun away inside his coat.

Natalie said, "I take it Chasseriau isn't at home."

"Nope," said Gomez. "The evidence indicates that he has flown in some haste. I don't think he was snatched."

Natalie poked her pretty chin with her forefinger. "I'm wondering."

"About what, Nat?"

"Whether or not," she said, "I should tell you what it is that's been bothering poor Mr. Chasseriau."

≡ 18 ≡

EARLY IN THE morning the Barset-London express had deposited Dan at the Marylebone Station, which stood in a secure section of the great city. There was a thick gray fog lying over Marylebone Road as he started making his way along it. The half dozen gilded robots, dressed in nineteenth-century costumes and singing Xmas carols in front of a squat brix church, looked insubstantial and sounded faraway.

Dan adjusted his muffler, then took yet another look at the slip of paper Jillian Kearny had given him. He'd consulted a map at one of the village shops and he knew he had to get over to the Edgware Road and then follow Park Lane along the border of Hyde Park. From there he'd have to find a way to slip into the unsecure zone where Nancy had gone.

"At least I think that's where she must've gone." Dan, hands deep in his trouser pockets,

141

walked determinedly along the quiet, misty streets of early morning London.

He was aware that he was sort of trying to imitate his father, that he was trying to be a detective. Yet he really didn't have that much confidence in himself. Sure, he'd acted brave and wise in front of Jillian, but he sometimes had doubts that he could handle this.

He wasn't even certain Nancy was really here in London someplace. If he did find her, he wondered if he would be able to persuade her to come back to Barsetshire with him.

The one thing he was sure of was that he had to try to find her. He had to see her again.

Following him through the blurred morning was the person who'd been tailing him since last night. A person who was betting that Nancy Sands was indeed in London and that Dan Cardigan would lead the way straight to her.

A short distance beyond Hyde Park Dan encountered a weathered barricade built of faded neowood planks and rusted barbed wire. Stenciled on it in shaky white letters were the words GANGZONE! KEEP OUT! EXTREME DANGER! Scanning the barrier, he noticed there'd once been a forcefence in operation here, too, but the projectors for that were broken and corroded.

He was thinking about trying to climb over the five-foot fence, wondering if he could do that without getting all snarled in the spiky wire, when a raspy voice behind him spoke.

"Away from there, m'lad," it warned, "or it'll be deep trouble you'll be getting into."

Standing nearby, broad gunmetal chest misted by the fog, was a large robot bobby. He had a truncheon built into his right hand and a stunrod in his left.

"I was only looking at it, officer," Dan told him in a tone he hoped sounded polite. "I'm— you know—a tourist."

"From America by the sound of you," said the copbot. "Well, this isn't a safe place for any tourist. Scoot along home to your hotel—off with you now!"

"Yes, sir. Sorry." Giving the robot a casual salute, Dan walked away.

As soon as he was out of sight of the mechanical man and shielded by the heavy fog, he began exploring the area. There were barricades blocking all of the streets leading into the zone dominated by the kid gangs. Finally, though, near Belgrave Square, he spotted a narrow lane where the barrier had recently been smashed down.

Dan went darting into the lane, the thick morning fog seeming to close in on him.

In the first block the buildings were gutted and empty. A soft, damp silence filled the street. Though he struggled to fight against it, Dan started shivering as he walked along. He found he was moving more slowly, his head turning from side to side to scan the dead, silent structures that floated in the fog.

He stepped on something, slipping, almost losing his balance.

What he'd put his foot down on was the severed head of a cat. Its dead eyes were open and staring, its teeth were bared in a rigid grimace.

Shaking himself as though he'd suddenly been splashed with something cold, Dan increased his pace.

He began noticing smells now. The pungent reek of potcigs, the strong odor of cooking fat, the smell of rotting flesh. Then he saw a child, a sexless kid of two or three, leaning in the gaping doorway of a ruined apartment house. Staring straight ahead, wide-eyed, with a bloody knife dangling in its pudgy fist.

From some of the buildings came the sounds of squabbling, lovemaking, fighting, laughing.

There were young people lounging on some of the porches, thin kids in their early teens, wearing patchwork outfits that didn't fit. They showed little interest in Dan's passing.

He turned another corner, cried out, stopped in his tracks.

There was the body of a naked girl of about sixteen lying in the street. Five large scruffy mongrel dogs were feeding on the corpse.

"Get away, get away!" shouted Dan, charging at them.

He was afraid it was Nancy.

But then he noticed that this girl was dark-haired and thin.

One of the dogs, a one-eyed gray with a

bloody muzzle, slowly turned. It began snarling warningly at him.

Dan felt he had to scare the animals off, then see about getting the girl's body to a safe place.

Another dog noticed him. It didn't growl or bristle. It simply charged at him, trying to sink its jagged teeth into his leg.

Dan stumbled back, went down on one knee, and then scuttled across the pavement.

The dog, a battered black mutt, missed his leg, wheeled to charge again.

Dan managed to scramble to his feet. He looked around desperately for something to use as a weapon. There was a board lying in the gutter and he snatched it up. Gripping it like a bat, he swung as the dog leaped again for him.

The wood connected with the animal's skull. There was a loud crackling noise. The dog yelped, whimpered as it fell to the ground. It lay still.

Two more of the wild dogs abandoned the dead girl to turn their attention to Dan.

"Get back!" He swung the board from side to side, causing it to whistle through the misty morning air. "Get back, damn it!"

The snarling animals hesitated, watching him.

Dan took a few slow steps backwards.

The dogs stayed where they were.

He tried a few more steps. Then he spun, started running away from them.

Someone, up in an unseen window, laughed.

* * *

Dan emerged from a dirty, twisty alley and into a commotion. Less than a half block away fifteen or more teens were circling a large, slow-moving robot. The bot had originally been enameled white and had the words BUREAU OF WELFARE STATISTICS lettered on his dented, dirt-smeared chest.

The kids, boys and girls, were whacking at the robot with lengths of hardplaz pipe, wooden clubs, and hunks of metal. That produced echoing bongs and bangs.

The metal man, oblivious, continued on his slow way along the street. "I'm only here to help you hooligans," he said in his deep, rumbling voice.

"We don't trust you, Stats!"

"You work for them."

Dan stopped, watching the fracas and trying to figure out what was going on.

Stats told the group, "All you whelps have to do is answer a few simple questions."

"Get back to your own zone."

"Skarf yourself, Stats."

A long, thin, black girl with orange hair took a swing at the robot with a rusty iron rod. She hit him square in his metal face.

"If you won't answer questions," explained the bot patiently, "there'll be no dole for you."

Just then the tip of a sharp blade poked into Dan's back.

"It'd be best, love, if you just come along quiet," suggested a whispering voice.

— ≡ 19 ≡ —

ARTHUR BAIRNHOUSE'S DESK was made of real
wood and was at least two centuries old. It was
piled high with folders, sheets of faxpaper,
memos, clippings, photos. The plump detective
was sitting behind it in a real wood chair.
"One of our operatives," he was telling Jake,
"just talked to a young woman named Jillian
Kearny. She goes to school in Barsetshire and
knows your son. She admits to having talked
to him immediately prior to his having run
away."

Jake asked, "Does she have any idea where
Dan went?"

"She passed on some information as to the
possible whereabouts of the Sands girl. She's
now very much afraid that Daniel disregarded
her warnings and came to London." From the
desktop clutter Bairnhouse picked up a map
and spread it out on a small cleared area.

"Take a look at this, if you will, Cardigan. This entire circled section of our city is a gang-ridden wilderness. Along here, at the end of Victoria Street, is the bailiwick of a youth gang that calls itself the Westminster Gang."

"They're near Westminster Abbey."

"Near the ruins of the abbey," said the plump detective. "According to Miss Kearny, the Sands girl has a friend who's a member of this particular gang. That friend's name in the civilized world was Mary Elizabeth Joiner. Now she's known as Silverhand Sally."

"Jillian Kearny told Dan that Nancy went to join this friend?"

Bairnhouse nodded. "She wanted him merely to pass the information on to the authorities—or to you. So that a search could be made for Nancy Sands. She apparently doesn't trust the people the Sands girl is living with, a couple named McCay. Your son, however, chose to hunt for his missing friend himself, it seems."

"That's like him, yeah."

"And like you, Cardigan," pointed out Bairnhouse. "Let's continue with this briefing, if you will. Here on the map you'll notice Grosvenor Place. That's where, in the shadow of what's left of Buckingham Palace, the Tek Kids are headquartered."

"Tek Kids?"

"Perhaps you haven't encountered them yet in America, or perhaps they're called something else." Bairnhouse rubbed at his flat nose. "TKs are the unfortunate offsprings of Tek-using mothers. They suffer from the mutagenic effects that prolonged use of Tek seems to have on a certain percentage of addicts."

"I think I did see a couple of reports on them," recalled Jake. "They tend to be extremely violent, amoral, vicious, and very quick to anger."

"Right you are. Too restless for school and virtually untreatable in institutions," said Bairnhouse, his thick forefinger tapping on the map. "What happens usually is that they gradually drift into the slums, ghettos, and ruins of our big cities. They form packs, and when they're not fighting amongst themselves, they prey on other gangs and pull off raids on the outside world. They unfortunately differ from other teen gangs in that a certain percentage of them have psionic powers. Some are teleks, others possess ESP powers. All of which makes TKs very dangerous, not the sort of people for either your son or yourself to become involved with."

Jake was studying the map. "The TKs aren't that far from the Westminsters."

"Exactly, and to reach Silverhand Sally your son may try to cross the TKs' sacred ground."

Jake grinned briefly. "I know, Arthur, that you're trying to discourage me from going in alone after Dan," he told the detective. "Your lecture, though, has the opposite effect. I can't let Dan wander around in there alone."

"I thought that would be your position, Cardigan."

"There's no alternative, since I understand the police are reluctant to cross over into that part of London."

"They make occasional trips," said Bairnhouse. "We might be able to persuade them to mount a search for your son and the Sands girl."

"After considerable red tape and circumlocution."

"They wouldn't undertake the job today, let us say."

"I'll do it alone."

From his desk Bairnhouse picked up a sheet of faxpaper. "Here's a small list of people who can provide you information, and dire warnings in some instances, about this part of London," he said, handing Jake the page. "I've also included a couple of reliable contacts who live in the gangzone."

Jake said, "Thanks, Arthur."

"We'll continue to work on this in our way, of course."

"Good. I'll continue to work on it in my way."

Natalie Dent was sitting in a silvery control chair in Briefing Room 2 of the Paris offices of

Newz, Inc. "Pay attention, Gomez," she urged. "Sit up straight."

He was slumped in a lower chair at her right, more or less watching the wall in front of them. It contained sixteen large pixmonitor screens, laid out in rows of four. "I've been drinking all this in, Nat," he assured her. "Hoping against hope that we'd soon get to the point."

"Once a putz always a putz," observed Sidebar. The robot cameraman was sitting in a fat chair at the rear of the big, chill room.

"What I've showed you thus far, which you ought to have comprehended, Gomez, is all important background material for what I'm about to reveal," said the red-haired reporter. "Is it perhaps that you're mooning over Mrs. Bouchon, who's not totally unattractive for a woman of her advanced years and—"

"Madeleine hasn't advanced anywhere near as far as I have, *chiquita.*"

"I couldn't help noticing, and you don't have to be a topflight investigative reporter such as I am to have spotted it, that she was quite profusely demonstrative and affectionate when you left her at that safe house your detective agency arranged for her."

"To a fiery Latin such as myself, Nat, a chaste peck on the forehead isn't considered the height of physical passion. Can we get to what you know about Michel Chasseriau?"

"What we're leading up to, Gomez, is exactly—"

"What did the guy want to impart to Madeleine Bouchon?"

"Really, Gomez. You're as grumpy as a bear with a sore nose."

"Paw."

"Beg pardon?"

"Sore paws are what, traditionally, make bears grumpy."

Natalie sighed. "Look at Screen 5," she suggested. "That's some footage of Bram Wexler, a Britisher who heads up the Paris office of the International Drug Control Agency." The smiling man on the monitor screen was in his early forties, conservatively dressed, strolling down a bright springtime Parisian boulevard completely unaware that he was being photographed. "Wexler was Bouchon's boss, and in the course of investigating all aspects of this story, I came across a tip that he may have some connection with Bouchon's murder."

"Where does Chasseriau come in?"

"He's been avoiding the office since the killing, uncertain as to what to do about the knowledge he has," answered the reporter. "Another informant told me that Chasseriau might be willing to talk about what he knew. That's Chasseriau on Screen 7."

On the monitor screen a frail young man in his middle twenties had appeared. He was nervously pacing the small living room of his apartment.

"Notice the quality of this footage," said Sidebar. "I shot it this morning, using nothing but natural light."

Gomez poked Natalie in the side with his thumb. "You folks called on him—and talked with him?"

"Bright and early," she replied.

"Can you tell me some of what he told you?"

"Bouchon had confided in him, just a few days before he was slaughtered, that he suspected Bram Wexler was conspiring with two or three of the major Teklords."

"That's a pretty serious charge. Did Bouchon have proof?"

"No, he wasn't even certain what exactly was going on, but he knew Wexler was involved in something shady and that it had to do with Tek," answered the redheaded reporter. "Originally, Bouchon had been sharing his suspicions with Zack Rolfe, calling on him at his place after office hours."

"*Bueno*. That means Bouchon wasn't fooling around and that Rolfe was lying."

"That seemed to me obvious from the start, Gomez, and I'm really astounded that none of the IDCA people, nor any of the policemen on this case, realized that," she said. "Gradually Bouchon began to wonder if he could trust Zack Rolfe. He apparently didn't much like Chasseriau, but he was certain he was honest.

So he came to him to discuss what was worrying him."

Gomez shook his head. "It was too late by
then. They'd already decided to kill Bouchon
to keep him from nosing around further."

"Now take a look at Screen 3." She touched
another button on the arm of the control chair.

A bland chinless man, wearing rich, regal
robes and a glittering, gem-encrusted golden
crown, was addressing a crowded auditorium.

"I'm keeping the sound off on all these images because it interferes with my narration,"
explained Natalie, "but you can take my word
that his powers of—"

"Caramba," said Gomez, "that's none other
than King Arthur II."

"Bram Wexler, a hypocrite who outwardly
pretends to be loyal to the President of Great
Britain, is associated with an organization
known as the Excalibur Movement," said Natalie. "Their prime objective is to see that England once again becomes a monarchy. I
haven't been able to find out yet if they'd resort to murder to gain their ends, but, by whatever means, they want to see this simp ruling
their country."

"This explains Zack Rolfe's last words."

"He said something to Jake as he was dying?
It would've been nice, Gomez, and in keeping
with your alleged newfound spirit of cooperation, had you found it in your peanut-sized
heart to share those words."

"Chiquita, what Rolfe did was warn Jake to watch out for Excalibur—or words to that effect."

The pretty reporter tapped the palms of her hands on her knees, then rubbed her hands together and smiled at him. "I can really sense this, we're on top of a very big story here."

"And a very big conspiracy most likely, involving Teklords, monarchists, and lord knows who else."

"It would make sense, especially since your partner is over in England just now, for you and I to work closely together on this from here on out, Gomez."

"Sí, absolutely," he said. "That's a dandy notion, Nat."

"Wonderful." Leaning over, she kissed him on the cheek.

"Mush," said Sidebar.

—≡ 20 ≡—

THERE HAD BEEN two of them, both carrying highly polished electroknives. When Dan had tried to explain to them what he was doing in the ruins, one of them slapped him hard across the face.

"We don't want any bleeding backtalk, puffer," he warned in his whispery voice. "You just keep it buttoned and come along with us, hear."

"But I'm—"

"What did I tell you about talking back?" The lanky blond young man slapped Dan again.

This blow hit him across the mouth, splitting his lip and drawing blood. Spitting, Dan started at the young man.

The other boy, who was thin and at least a year younger than Dan, stepped between them. "He doesn't mean any harm, Ludd," he said, catching hold of Dan's arm and shoving him back.

"Let him try to come at me, Angel. I'd like a chance to slice his heart out."

"No, we have to take him back to camp. That's the rules."

"Rules, my arse." Ludd swung his knife up in front of his face, flicking the switch that started the sawtooth blade whirring. "What's to stop us from slitting him open here and now, taking his dabs, and—"

"That's against the rules," warned Angel. "Strangers have to be taken to camp. After that, if Jamaica decides, we can kill him."

"Whole blooming country's going to hell because of bloody rules." He slashed angrily at the air with his knife, shut it off, and jammed it into his thigh holster. "All right, all right, we'll act like raving twits and take him back with us."

Angel knuckled Dan's upper arm. "It isn't a far walk," he told him quietly. "Don't try to break loose, don't say a bleeding word—otherwise Ludd may decide to do for you."

After a few seconds, Dan nodded curtly.

After leaving the detective agency offices, Jake walked along Berkeley Street. As the day waned, it grew grayer and colder and a harsh wind filled the crowded walkways. The skytrams flying slowly overhead were brightly decorated for the holiday season, each one playing a different Xmas tune from the speakers planted in its red and green underside.

Stationed on the corner was a chrome-plated newsbot, hawking the *Daily Skan*. Jake paused, seemingly to listen to the mechanical man recite the menu of scandalous news to be found in this afternoon's edition.

"Is the VP a puff?" asked the bot in his deep tinny voice. "Who caught Senator Yates-Drake with his trousers down? Are there Martians living in Manchester? Whose knickers were found in the War Sec's skyvan?"

A plump black man brushed by Jake. "Excuse me, sir," he said, poking his Banx card into the appropriate slot in the robot's side.

"Here's a bloke what knows what's news." Whirring and rattling, the robot swiftly produced an eight-page faxcopy of the *Skan* out of the wide slot across his chest. "Here you are, guv, hot off the blooming presses."

As the customer accepted his newspaper, Jake moved on. He was certain now, as he'd suspected since leaving Bairnhouse's, that he was being tailed. Crossing the street, he went through one of the arched entryways to the Berkeley Square Multimall.

It was exceedingly warm on the ground level of the vast mall, and the air smelled of pine boughs and hot toddy. Jake hopped onto a servoramp and let it start him on a slow circuit of the place. He rode by a string of selfserve boutiques—Stylz, Fitz, Ragz—and then past a

great, sprawling food market called Farmer
Dell's Hydroponic Farmstand, Branch #225 of
My Man Chumley's Fish & Chips and Branch
#316 of Pubz, Inc. He stepped off the moving
ramp in front of the St. George & The Dragon
Inn. The neowood sign dangling over the wide
doorway of the simulated country inn offered a
crude depiction of the armored saint slaying a
fierce, fire-breathing creature. The paint was
convincingly aged to make it seem centuries
old.

Jake ignored the main entrance, slipping instead into the imitation courtyard next to the
imitation inn. The yard was paved with au-
thentic-looking cobblestones, and a wagon
loaded with real straw was parked near the
simulated stables.

Running, Jake stationed himself behind the
wagon. He couldn't be seen from here, but he
had a good view of the entrance of the courtyard.

Within the shadowy stables robot horses
snorted and shifted on their hooves. Even the
smell of a real stable, suitably subdued, came
drifting out of the shadows.

A moment passed before a figure slipped,
cautiously, into the courtyard.

It was a slim young woman, auburn-haired,
in her late twenties. She was the one Jake had
noticed following him. She might be with Scotland Yard, yet he doubted that.

When she was a few feet from the stable

door, he eased out from behind the wagon and poked the barrel of his stungun into her back.

Dan had seen what was left of the vast Westminster Abbey rising up out of the fog. The remains of the Gothic structure lay dead ahead across a wide, weedy field that was pocked with craters and dotted with scrubby brush and a few stunted trees. Most of its nearest tower was gone and there were great gaps in the stone walls.

Dozens of sooty pigeons were circling the abbey in a restless way.

Ludd held up his hand and halted. "Bollocks," he muttered, moving behind a gnarled tree midway across the field.

Angel stopped, too, yanking Dan over beside him. "Something's bloody wrong." He was squinting up at the pigeons as they circled in the foggy sky.

Whipping out his knife, Ludd said, "Something's gone and got them bleeding birds all excited." Uneasiness sounded in his voice.

"I'll slip closer," offered Angel, letting go of Dan, "to see what's going on."

Ludd shook his head. "No, you stay here with the ponce," he ordered. "I'll do the bloody reconnoitering."

"Hell, I'm smaller and quicker."

"Stick here." Ducking low, Ludd started a zigzag course across the field.

Dan asked Angel, "What do you think's wrong?"

He was watching his buddy move closer to the ruined abbey. "Could be most anything," he answered as the fog swallowed up Ludd. "But those pigeons being agitated like that, it definitely means something must be going on wrong at our camp."

"Westminster is your camp?"

"I just said that, didn't I now?"

"But I'm looking for the Westminster Gang."

"That's not too smart, since we don't take kindly to visitors," said Angel. "Or tourists."

"Is there a girl named Silverhand Sally with you?"

"How'd you know that name?"

"Somebody told me to ask for her. Is she here?"

"Sal might be or she might not." He turned to scrutinize Dan. "Why do you want our Sal?"

"Because I'm hoping she can help me find a friend of mine—girl named Nancy Sands."

"Ar, I see."

"Do you know Nancy? Is she at the abbey?"

Before Angel could answer, there was a shout from up ahead in the fog. "Been a damned raid!" yelled Ludd through cupped hands. "Get your arse over here, Angel. There's a lot of people dead."

162

—≡21≡—

"Now HERE'S WHAT you do," suggested Jake. "Very slowly and carefully, turn around. Then explain why the hell you've been tailing me."

The pretty, auburn-haired young woman was smiling when she faced him. "I underestimated you," she said, rubbing the toe of her boot across the imitation flagstones of the inn courtyard. "You'll have to forgive me. I guess taking care of myself over in the gangzones has made me a trifle too confident."

"You're not with the police?"

"No, the Welfare Squad," she explained. "I'm Marj Lofton."

"Oh, so?"

"Beth Kittridge suggested that I look you up."

"Really?"

"Didn't she tell you about me? Beth implied that she had. We're old friends from SoCal Tech days."

In the stable one of the robot horses whinnied.

Jake took a careful step backwards, keeping his stungun aimed at her. "Show me your ID packet."

"Sure." She slid her hand into a jacket pocket. "I was going to introduce myself to you in a minute. Honest."

He accepted the proffered IDs, glanced through them. "Why trail me at all?"

"Showing off. I was anxious to impress you."

After handing the packet back, Jake slipped his gun away. "Why?"

Marj said, "Beth told me, when she called a couple hours ago, that she thought I might be able to help you. But she also warned me that you're very independent, a true loner."

Jake grinned. "Nope, I'm actually a team player from way back," he assured the young woman. "Thing is, I have to be captain of the team and pick all my crew."

"Fair enough," Marj said. "Do you know for certain that your son's over in gang territory?"

"There's a very strong possibility," he answered. "He's trying to find his missing girlfriend and she's supposed to be holed up with the Westminsters."

Frowning, Marj shook her head. "A very rough bunch," she observed. "Why'd the girl pick them?"

"A friend of hers apparently runs with the gang. Kid they call Silverhand Sally."

"Yes, I know Sal. For a while I even thought she might be salvable."

"You don't think that anymore?"

"Oh, it's still possible maybe, but the odds are getting longer."

Jake said, "I'd like to go over there soon as I can."

"Could you use a guide?"

"I could use a good one," Jake told her. "But I don't want anybody who's trying too hard to impress me. Somebody who's more interested in showboating than in getting the job done."

"I'm sorry I stalked you," she said. "Most days I'm not like that."

"When can we leave?"

"I have to gather up some stuff for the trip," Marj said. "Suppose I meet you at your hotel in two hours?"

"Okay, fine." He held out his hand.

Shaking it, she said, "I really am pretty good."

"I'm counting on that," he said.

The Parisian night was crisp and clear. Hands in the pockets of the stylish thermocoat he'd purchased earlier in the day, Gomez was strolling along beside the dark Seine. He'd found over the years that solitary walks sometimes helped him think.

"Muy frio," he remarked to himself. "Being a crackerjack international investigator has

its disadvantages. One of which is frigid climes."

On the night river a music barge was slowly sailing by. A band of brightly uniformed robot musicians was playing a solemn Xmas carol. The golden glitter of their uniform trim sparkled and flashed in the illumination from the boat's multicolor tubelights.

Gomez continued along parallel to the boat for a few minutes. Then, turning his back to it, he walked away from the river and headed in the direction of his hotel.

"I have a hunch that various events, including some of what's afoot in England with Jake's offspring, ought to tie together," he reflected. "But, *madre,* I still don't see quite how."

He chose a different route than the one he'd traveled on his way to the Seine and just off the Place du Châtelet he spotted someone who looked vaguely familiar. The man was walking hurriedly along, coming toward Gomez on the opposite side of the street.

"Who the hell is that *hombre?*" the detective asked himself, feigning indifference.

Then, snapping his fingers without taking his hand out of his pocket, he realized who it was.

The man hurrying now up the stone steps of a narrow apartment building across the way was Bram Wexler, the head of the Paris office of the International Drug Control Agency and the guy Natalie Dent had just been showing him pictures of. He was the one their client's late husband had suspicions about.

Gomez glanced, quickly and casually, around. He spotted a recessed doorway that was very sparsely lit. He entered it, striving to look innocent, and took up a watchful position.

The night grew colder.

Gomez turned up the controls on his coat, but then the garment started giving off a burning plaz smell. He turned the controls down again.

Fifteen chill minutes later, the IDCA man came out of the building. He was accompanied by a plump woman of forty-some years. The two of them walked to the end of the block and got into a parked landcar.

"Chihuahua," commented Gomez. "I know that lady. In fact I once enjoyed a broken leg because of her. What the devil is she doing in Paris? And why's she hobnobbing with this lad?"

Gomez was hunched in the vidphone alcove, a glass of ale in his left hand, talking to a robot. He was in the living room of the suite at the Louvre Hotel and the bot was in the Data Center of the Cosmos Detective Agency in Greater Los Angeles.

"Nothing out of the ordinary on Dr. Hilda Danenberg," the silvery mechanical man was telling him. "Her record seems to be, as always, spotless."

"Why's she in Paris?"

"Vacation, it says here."

"She's hanging around with a lad name of Bram Wexler, who's—"

"Head of the Paris office of the IDCA," supplied the infobot. "According to our sources they're just friends."

"And she's got no official reason for keeping company with Wexler? The IDCA didn't send for her?"

"Nope."

Pausing, Gomez took a sip of his ale. "Is the lady still in contact with Professor Kittridge?"

"They're no longer on friendly— Oops, wait now, Gomez. Here's something," said the robot. "Dr. Danenberg has made three visits to the Bay Area in NorCal in recent weeks. And—"

"Yeah, that's where Kittridge is at work on his long-awaited anti-Tek system. Any indication that she dropped in on the prof?"

"None, but it's still a possibility, isn't it? Her activities, keep in mind, weren't that closely monitored."

Nodding, Gomez said, "Okay, thanks."

"De nada," said the robot. "That's a little bit of Mexican lingo I—"

"I noticed. *Gracias.*" Ending the conversation, he left the phone alcove.

He was standing at the window, gazing out

at nothing in particular, when the door announced, "A Miss Dent to see you."

"Oy," observed the detective, turning to frown at the door. "Yeah, all right, let her in."

Natalie came in carrying a vidcaz clutched in her right hand. "I thought, since we're allegedly working side by side and shoulder to shoulder on this mess, that you'd enjoy viewing what Sidebar has just shot."

"He's not going to drop in, too, is he?"

"No, he went over to the—"

"Bueno. Make yourself to home, dear lady," he invited with moderate enthusiasm. "My *casa* is yours and so on."

Ignoring the chair he was pointing at, the reporter walked over and thrust the vidcaz into a slot in the wall. "You'll find, I'm near certain, that this footage is most interesting."

"Did you have something sour for dinner?"

"I didn't, truth to tell, manage even to have dinner, since I've been much too busy tracking down leads."

"You're wearing a rather grim expression on your usually lovely puss, *chiquita,* and I thought perhaps you'd ingested something that—"

"I tend to take on a glum look whenever I'm in your vicinity, Gomez. Now, please, shut your yap, and watch."

A familiar stretch of Parisian thoroughfare blossomed on the vidwall. Walking rapidly along it was Bram Wexler. The camera followed him down the street and up the steps of Dr. Hilda Danenberg's apartment. The sound of his footfalls came out of the wallspeakers.

"Nice bit of cinematography," commented Gomez.

Then, blown up large on the wall, appeared Gomez himself. He was hunched in the recessed doorway and watching the Danenberg apartment.

"Some operative you are," said Natalie. "You're about as obvious as an elephant in a china shop, and you stick out, if you don't mind my mentioning the fact, like a sore finger or a—"

"Thumb."

"What?"

"People tend to stand out like sore thumbs," he said. "And it's bulls, not elephants, who create havoc in china shops."

"Well, an elephant wouldn't be all that inconspicuous either, but that's not the issue at hand."

"You say Sidebar snapped this stuff?"

"He did, yes."

"He's very unobtrusive. I never suspected that he was—"

"That's what good surveillance is all about. The trick, and I should think you'd be aware of that by now, since you've spent untold years as an alleged snooper, the trick is not to allow anyone to notice you." She watched the wall as Dr. Danenberg and Wexler drove away.

"Simpleton that I am, Gomez, I persist in giving you the benefit of the doubt and therefore I'm assuming that you were intending, eventually, to share with me the insights you gathered from this clumsy shadowing job."

"Clumsy it wasn't," he corrected. "I was quite cunning and deft, considering that I had to improvise. Bumping into Wexler purely by chance, I—"

"Oh, really now. Don't try to con me into believing that you didn't even know—"

"Es verdad," he insisted. "Absolutely true that I encountered that *hombre* by chance and decided to tail him."

She eyed him up and down. "You really weren't aware he was going to call on Dr. Danenberg?"

"I wasn't even aware the dear lady was in Paree. Last time I heard, she was in far-off Greater LA."

"But you worked on a case involving her. It was, in fact, the first case that Jake Cardigan handled for Cosmos. You teamed up right after he was sprung from the Freezer prison through the machinations of your boss, Walt Bascom, and—"

"Nat, I don't keep in touch with all the folks I've bumped into on cases over the years. We don't have annual reunions, don't even exchange Xmas cards." He finished his ale. "Actually, you know, I never met the doctor herself but only an android sim. When the damn thing chanced to blow up, I executed an impromptu somersault off a sunny boardwalk and ended up with a busted leg."

Natalie gave him a brief look of sympathy. "Yes, I recall hearing about that incident," she said. "Just one more example of how clumsy you can be at times. However, we'd better forget your past foul-ups and concentrate on—"

"Do you happen to know why Dr. Danenberg's in town?"

"Not yet, though I expect we—"

"You are aware that she used to be both an associate and a ladyfriend of Professor Kittridge?"

Nodding, Natalie said, "Yes, and I'm trying to find out if she's still in contact with him."

"*Sí,* that would be worth knowing," agreed Gomez, studying the ornate ceiling.

"What we also have to learn is why she's seeing Wexler, a man who's probably in cahoots with the Tek cartels."

Gomez smiled broadly. "I think I'll drop in on the lady."

"That might be too obvious, a tipoff that we're suspicious of her."

"Not the way I'll handle it," he assured her. "You've apparently never seen the subtle, clever side of my character at work."

"But I have," Natalie said. "That's what worries me."

—═22═—

THE LEADER OF the Westminsters had knocked
Dan down. "I've got no time for this asshole
now," he'd told Ludd and Angel.

Crouched against a pile of rubble, Dan
asked, "Where's Nancy Sands?"

Angel dropped down next to him. "Shut up
now," he advised.

"Is she dead?"

"Take it easy. We don't know who all's dead
yet."

He'd been brought inside the lofty abbey.
Carved stone walls rose up high on three sides.
The fourth wall of this section had long since
fallen away, and you could see the weedy, potted field they'd just crossed.

"Bastards," the lean, black young man who
headed the gang was saying. "Goddamn TKs.
Swooped down, using all those freak tricks of
theirs. Killing, smashing."

Sprawled across the wide expanse of mosaic floor were at least a dozen bodies.

Dan, hunched, started moving from corpse to corpse.

Nancy was not among them.

"Buggers took stuff, too," the black Jamaica told Ludd. "Looted us."

"They always do that."

"It was worse this time, goddamn it. They carried off the bleeding Coronation Chair—and the Stone of Scone."

"What the hell they want with that?"

"Maybe they're planning to crown some bugger king," said the angry Jamaica. "Maybe they just want to take turns sitting on the fucker."

Dan made his way back to where Angel was standing. "How can I find out about Nancy?"

Angel caught hold of his arm. "They probably took the injured into the Cloisters," he said quietly. "We can go look there first off."

They'd moved only a few steps when Jamaica noticed them. "Where you taking that bugger?"

"I'm just going to—"

"Who the hell is he, anyway?"

"Outsider," put in Ludd. "Tourist bloke. We caught him and brought him here to see what valuables he—"

"Just kill him," instructed Jamaica. "We've got no time for him. Later you can go through his pockets and—"

174

"Wait now." Dan broke free of Angel's grip and walked up to the leader. "I'm not a damned tourist, I'm here looking for Nancy Sands. I didn't come here to do you any harm or—"

"Shut up right now."

"Is Silverhand Sally around?" asked Dan.

Jamaica was sliding a snubnosed lazgun out of his thigh holster. "You know Sal?"

"Nancy does, and so—"

"Jamaica, it won't hurt to let him chat a bit with our Sal," put in Angel. "After that, if she doesn't know him, then we can kill him off. Okay?"

Jamaica dropped the weapon back into its holster. After rubbing his palm across his crimson tunic, he said, "All right, okay. She's in the nave. Take him there and if he makes any trouble on the way, he's dead and done for."

"All I want is—"

"He won't make any trouble," promised Angel, tugging at Dan's arm. When they were walking along a dim, vaulted corridor, he said, "That was very risky, getting beaky with Jamaica. He's not a chap who's too awfully fond of debating."

"Yeah, I know that, but—"

"You on the other hand truly love to argue."

Dan nodded. "Guess I do, yeah."

There were seven or eight young people in the large, stone-walled room Angel brought him to. Three of them had been wounded and were bandaged. None of them was Nancy.

Silverhand Sally finished bandaging the third and turned toward Angel. She was a slim girl of about seventeen, blonde, wearing tan trousers, a gray tunic, and a gunbelt that held two lazguns. Her right hand and arm to the elbow were of silvery metal. "Who's that with you?"

"I'm Dan Cardigan." He crossed the mosaic floor to her. "You're a friend of Nancy's and—"

"Dan Cardigan." She stood. "Sure, she told me about you."

"I figured she might be staying with you, so I came to find her," he explained. "Where is she?"

Sally shook her head. "I'm sorry, Dan. The Tek Kids took some prisoners," she said quietly. "Nancy was one of them."

Sally, her chill metallic hand holding his arm, was leading Dan along a shadowy, vaulted corridor. They were moving away from the cookfires, and darkness started to close in. The intricate carvings on the stone walls and the ornate wooden ornamentation were barely discernible. "You should've eaten," she told him.

"Not very hungry."

"Dog meat's not bad," the blonde young woman said. "Takes a bit of getting used to. Mostly, though, that's because in the world you and I come from, we think of them only as pets."

"You ever going to go back?"

"Mind that fallen masonry, scrunch over close to this wall," she cautioned. "No, I'm here for life."

"Why?"

"Because this is better than that was."

"Parents?"

"Father mostly." She guided him through an arched doorway. "After my accident, after I got my imitation arm, he turned much worse. Not that he was ever a very good dad."

Dan asked her, "The arm you have now— that's not the one they got you originally, is it?"

"Oh, no, not at all. No, they bought me a very proper, very conventional one. Highly believable and looking just exactly like flesh and blood. Duck your head for a minute along here and keep an eye cocked for bats," she warned as they entered another long, partially ruined corridor. "Might be a few rats underfoot, too."

"So why the silver arm?"

"Well, I simply grew tired of the bullshit," she replied. "Seemed like every time I'd touch anybody with the replacement, they'd cringe or look all nervous. I decided, why hide the damn thing? I got me a nice shiny robot arm and now there's no question as to whether it's real or not. If I touch you, you know damn well

177

what I touched you with and fuck you if you don't like it."

They'd reached a room that was nearly intact. Statues and carvings ringed it.

Sally let go of him. "You can bunk safely here for tonight," she told him. "On one of those straw mats yonder." From under her tunic she produced a squat chunk of tallow candle. "Probably have the place to yourself, since most of them think it's haunted hereabouts. This used to be called the Poets' Corner." Lighting the candle, she stuck it down on a stone bench.

To his right Dan noticed a wall carving of someone referred to as "O rare Ben Jonson."

He asked, "What's likely to happen to Nancy?"

"Best not to think about it, Dan."

"I can't just let them—"

"It's tough, I know. But believe me, the TKs will kill you dead if you try to go near their digs at Buckingham Palace."

"But she's a friend of yours, too. How can—"

"Living here, being part of a gang, that means you can't afford to be sentimental."

"We're not talking about making stew out of dogs," he said to her, angry. "This is a girl who may be raped or tortured or even killed."

Sally touched his arm with her real fingers. "I'd like to help, but there's nothing to do," she said. "You saw what happened here, how many of us they hurt and killed."

"I thought gangs like yours believed in revenge."

"Sure, but not in suicide." She walked over, kicking at a sleeping mat with her foot. "Eventually we'll do something, you can count on that, but it'll be carefully planned."

"Meantime, Nancy's in danger."

"Yes, but that can't be helped," Sally said. "You'd best turn in now. I have to get back."

"Why'd she come here?"

"You already know that. Nancy was looking for some kind of sanctuary."

"No, I mean why did she run away from the McCays?"

"She didn't like them much."

"Maybe not, but her life wasn't in danger there and it sure as hell is here."

Sally said, "Well, she overheard some conversations."

"About what—her father?"

The girl nodded. "It's funny, you know, some girls take one hell of a long time to see through their dads," she said. "Nancy, in spite of everything, had been going along thinking that Bennett Sands was an innocent chap who'd been maligned and framed by the authorities." She laughed. "And him one of the Tek kingpins. But, you know, you couldn't get her to believe that."

Dan moved closer to her. "Why'd she change, what did she find out?"

"She didn't confide all that much in me,

Dan. But I know she happened to overhear the McCays talking about a business venture that was going to involve her father."

"A Tek business venture?"

"Exactly, and something quite big and important," answered Sally.

"How's he going to run Tek business from prison?"

"Maybe he's not planning to stay in prison. I'm not sure," she said. "All I know is that whatever Nancy overheard upset her a good deal. She had to get away from there for a while to think everything over."

"She could've come to me for help."

"I think eventually she was going to," said Sally. "Confide everything she'd learned to you and your dad. But, see, she still had a feeling that doing that would be betraying her father. That's why she wanted some time to make up her mind about just what to do. Of course, dear old pop had betrayed Nancy for years and thought nothing of it, but she didn't see things that way." Patting his arm, she leaned and kissed him on the cheek. "Bed down. I'll fetch you early in the morning and we'll see about getting you safely back to your own."

After a few seconds he answered, "Yeah, that'll be the best thing, I guess. Thanks, Sally."

She left him.

He looked around the Poets' Corner, at the

statues and carvings. "Longfellow, Chaucer," he recited absently. "Milton, Gray."

He sat on a straw mat for a while, watching the flickering flame on the fat candle.

When he figured it must be past midnight, he took up the candle and started back the way he'd come.

Soon he reached a break in the wall. Beyond showed foggy night. Extinguishing the candle, he set it carefully down on the stones. Then he slipped out into the darkness.

He was heading for Buckingham Palace.

Behind him in the fog a solitary figure followed.

—≡ 23 ≡—

A SLEETY RAIN was hitting against the leaded windows of the small cozy restaurant. A very convincing hologram fire seemed to be blazing cheerily in the simulated stone fireplace near their table.

Marj mentioned, "You're not eating."

Jake glanced down at his soup. "I don't seem to be, do I?"

Reaching across the table, she put her hand briefly on his. "I know you're anxious to get going, Jake. But, keep in mind, decent meals will be hard to come by over there."

"Is this part of some deal you made with Beth?"

Her eyes went wide. "You think she told me to look after you and make certain you ate at least one meal a day?"

"Yeah."

"Well, yes, she did," admitted the young

183

woman. "Detective work, after all, doesn't require fasting."

"I know, but I'm eager to get going."

"We'll find your son, don't worry." She reached down to pick up the shoulder bag she'd deposited on the imitation hardwood floor. "Here's a little gadget you'd better carry with you."

He accepted the small black disk that she took from her bag and handed to him. "Good-luck charm?"

Smiling, she told him, "It's something I developed myself—based on a somewhat larger one used by Scotland Yard."

"And it does what?"

"It serves as a sort of scrambler," Marj explained. "We may run into some Tek Kids over there, ones with ESP talent. This'll keep them from tapping in on what we're thinking."

Holding the disk between thumb and forefinger, he studied it for a moment before dropping it into his coat pocket. "The TKs really can do that sort of stuff?"

"Oh, yes. Some of them are very gifted in some pretty strange and unsettling ways."

"You say you came up with this gadget yourself?"

"I've long since given up my major calling, which was robotics. But I find I still like to tinker with small electronics projects now and then. Eat your soup."

"Oh, yeah." He took a few spoonfuls. "Why'd you change careers?"

"Why'd you?"

"Didn't have much choice."

"Well, in a way, neither did I. A few years ago I simply started feeling that I needed to work more directly with people," she explained. "Help them in some firsthand way."

"Designing and constructing androids helps."

"Sure, maybe. But I was simply getting too detached from the outside world. I quit and came over here. I'm much happier these days."

"That meant leaving family and friends to—"

"Oh, I've made new friends here in England," she assured him. "And I had no family left, not after my brother died."

Jake said nothing.

After a moment Marj spoke again. "Excuse my turning gloomy on you, Jake."

He asked, "You have contacts in the gang sectors, don't you?"

"Yes. People who'll see us safely along our way."

"Then we ought to be able to get through to Westminster Abbey tonight."

"If it's safe."

"Meaning?"

She said, "There's been a lot of feuding between gangs lately. Right now the Westminsters are having trouble with the TKs."

"Is this the kind of feuding where kids can get killed?"

"Almost always," she replied. "If there is any sort of skirmishing going on tonight, we may have to lie low until it's over."

"If Dan's in the middle of a gang war, I don't intend to wait around—"

"Jake, I know you're used to being in charge," she said. "But, really, you're going to have to trust me. I'll be able to tell you if it's safe to approach the abbey or not."

Finally he nodded. "You're right, yeah. You'll have to decide."

Their waiter, an extremely polite android, approached the table with a bottle of red wine. "Excuse me," he said, bowing. "I've been asked to bring this to you."

"Compliments of the house?" asked Jake.

"No, compliments of Denis Gilford." The pale reporter seated himself, uninvited, in the spare chair at their table. "One senses a big story brewing with you two in the thick of it. I demand all the details."

Gomez smiled as he held out the bouquet of plazroses. "Good evening, Dr. Danenberg," he said, handing her the fake flowers and striding on into her apartment. "We haven't actually met, but I once broke a leg because of you."

The plump woman looked crossly at him. "Oh, yes, you're . . . Sanchez, isn't it?"

"Close. Actually I'm Gomez," he explained,

smiling more broadly. "I'm with the Cosmos Detective Agency and because of a case we're working on, I thought perhaps—"

"How'd you know I was here?"

He fluffed the plyopillow on a rubberoid armchair and then seated himself. "Being an ace investigator, finding you wasn't particularly difficult."

"Actually, it doesn't matter, Mr. Gomez," she told him sternly. "The hour is late and—"

"The reason I'm intruding on you, doctor, is that you're an expert on Tek and on the anti-Tek system that Professor Kittridge is developing."

"I've had absolutely no contact with the man for quite some time now," she said. "If you need information on any aspect of the fight against Tek, I suggest you call on the International Drug Control Agency. They have an office right here in Paris."

"Ah, but that may not be a wise thing to do just now." He stood up. "We have reason to believe—and this is confidential info I'm confiding in you, doc—that some of the local IDCA officials may well be in cahoots with some of the Teklords." Gomez walked over to a wall to straighten a hanging triop picture of a field of yellow flowers.

"That's interesting," said Dr. Danenberg. "Yet, as I told you, I have no connection whatsoever with Professor Kittridge."

"What brings you to Paris?" He ran his hand

along the back of another armchair, then sat in it, crossed his legs, and smiled hopefully up at the plump woman.

"A vacation."

"And you haven't heard anything about, say, plans to sabotage Kittridge's work?"

"The professor and I didn't part under the best of circumstances," she said evenly.

"But you do know a lot about how this anti-Tek system of his works, don't you?"

"I know how it worked some time ago, though he may have modified it greatly since then," she answered, moving toward the door. "Basically his system is based on RF waves. Radio frequency waves emitted at a high oscillation rate. Once you find the exact oscillation rate, you can shatter any Tek chip in existence. When you broadcast that high-frequency RF from a powerful satellite station, you'd be able to destroy most of the world's supply of Tek chips all at once."

"If a Tek cartel, or a combo of same, could come up with a way to circumvent this upcoming electronic passover, cook up a chip that was immune, they'd have a very lucrative monopoly, wouldn't they?" He left his latest seat.

"Perhaps they would. I'm not, however, at all interested in the activities of the Tek cartels—or in your activities, Mr. Gomez. I'm afraid, considering the hour, that I must ask you to leave."

He sat down on the metallic sofa, rested his

arm on the sofa back for a moment. "You see, doctor, that case that Jake Cardigan and I are here working on—you do know Jake, don't you?"

"We've met. It was in Mexico, I believe."

"Jake and I are partners. He's the one who didn't break his leg."

"I assure you I'm sorry you were once injured, somewhat indirectly to be sure, because of me, yet—"

"We think there's a Tek angle to the murder we're investigating. I was hoping you'd be able to assist us."

"I can't help you in any way." She opened the door. "Good night now, Mr. Sanchez."

"Gomez." Smiling, he walked to the doorway. "Well, it's been jolly meeting you in person at long last. *Buenas noches.*"

He left her apartment, started whistling, walked to the corner, and turned onto a side street. He made his way to his rented landcar and climbed into the driveseat. "They working, *chiquita?*"

Natalie was sitting, slightly hunched, in the passenger seat and listening to a set of portable earphones. "Yessir, all the minbugs you planted seem to be functioning just fine," she informed him. "Dr. Danenberg, by the way, talks to herself."

"Many brilliant people do. Me, for instance."

"She's talking to herself about you right now. Want to hear?"

"Nope."

The reporter said, "I only agree with half the negative things she's saying about you."

"I'm eternally grateful for your support." He started the car.

$\equiv$ **24** $\equiv$

As DAN HAD gotten closer to the ruins of Buckingham Palace, the night had turned quiet. A thick fog hung over the rutted streets and overgrown parkland he was passing. Up ahead in the gray mist now he saw a winged figure floating high in the air, and below it a seated woman.

Slowing his pace, he moved cautiously closer.

This must be the Queen Victoria Memorial, which meant he was nearing the palace.

Chunks of stone and metal had fallen away from the memorial. Names and curses had been painted and etched across the figures.

"Isn't it awfully late for you to be up and around, Dan?"

He stopped still, staring up.

Perched near the feet of the seated queen was a thin, dark-haired girl. About eighteen, she wore a long, simple black dress.

"How'd you know my—"

"It's easy, love." She smiled and tapped at her temple with a slender forefinger. "I've got the gift, I do. My name is Morgana."

"And you claim you can read my thoughts?"

"Don't claim, love, can. With no trouble at all." Turning, she started climbing down to the ground. "You really think I'm too skinny?"

He brought his hand up to the side of his head. "Not exactly, but—"

"And that I'm nowhere near as pretty as Nancy?" She landed on the damp ground, shaking her head. "No, I am not a bitch. When you get to know me, why . . . Ah, but I'm being forgetful. You aren't going to have the opportunity of getting to know me."

"I have to find—"

"Dan, love, I know all that," cut in Morgana. She stood watching him, head tilted slightly to the left, hands clasped behind her back. "You fancy that you're on a lovely knightlike quest. Touching, that is."

"Is she here?"

"That's a very impressive school you attend," she told him. "What you have to do now, love, is turn right round and head yourself back for there. Should you survive to reach a safe part of this great bloody city, then you simply hop on a train for Bunter Academy." She took a few slow steps in his direction. "That's truly where you belong, my dear."

"I have to see Nancy, talk to her."

"That's quite impossible, Sir Daniel."

"No, damn it. If she's here with you people, then—"

"There's absolutely no way, truly, that you can help her," Morgana assured him. "You may think of yourself as the lady's champion, but you're really just a schoolboy, is all."

"Schoolboy or not, I'm going to—"

"Let me explain the situation a bit further, Dan, love," continued the thin, dark girl. "Lancelot, he's taken quite a fancy to this Nancy of yours, do you see? I really for the life of me can't understand why, but there it is."

"Who the hell is Lancelot? And why do you all have names out of the stories of King Arthur and his—"

"All you need to know, sweet, is that Lancelot is the head man," explained Morgana, bringing her arms in front of her and folding them across her chest. "As I said, Lancelot is smitten, and even as we speak, he's in one of the royal bedchambers with your Nancy, trying to convince her to—"

"I'm going in there."

"That you're not, love. Merlin!"

A heavyset young man with short-cropped blond hair materialized out of the fog. He had on a loose, tattered gray overcoat. "Told you he'd be too dumb to save his arse."

"I'm going to get inside there," Dan said. "If I have to fight you first, well, then, okay."

Merlin chuckled. "Oh, I say, Danny Boy," he

said, shaking his plump head. "I never *fight*."

"He doesn't have to," explained Morgana. "You may as well go ahead and do it, Merlin love. Don't, though, hurt him too much, you hear? He's got some really sweet notions in that cute little head of his."

Dan decided he'd better make his move before the thickset young man pulled out a weapon.

As he started for Merlin, the chunky young man raised his left hand and pointed at Dan.

All at once Dan felt his breath go whooshing out of his chest. Intense pain spread through his body.

His feet left the ground and he went rising up, in a zigzag way, through the thick night fog.

He slammed into the figure of Queen Victoria. Then he was yanked back. He spun around once before plummeting downward.

Dan smacked into the ground and passed out.

Their car on the underground tubetrain was rushing smoothly along, nearly empty.

"I'm surprised that Denis was so cooperative," said Marj. "When he first sat down with us, I was certain he was going to insist on coming along."

Jake grinned. "I persuaded him we didn't need a reporter."

"That usually doesn't discourage Denis. He and his paper are extremely persistent."

"And I'm extremely persuasive."

"After you suggested that the two of you talk things over privately in the alley, I expected a fight," she admitted. "That's the way the kid gangs settle things."

"No need for a fight."

She turned in her seat, studying his face. "I don't know you very well, Jake, but that looks like a smug expression on your face," she said. "What really took place in the alley?"

"I used my stungun on him."

"What? But that's not—"

"Sporting?"

"I don't mean that exactly. It's only that I thought you'd used reason on him and—"

"I had a chat with Gilford earlier. He didn't strike me as the sort of guy you could reason with."

"I see, yes."

"As I told you, Marj, the important thing to me is finding my son."

"So you used your gun."

"On its lowest setting. He'll only be out for an hour or so," Jake assured her. "And I propped him up in a comfortable, fairly warm spot."

"I'd forgotten that yours is a violent profession."

"It is," he agreed. "If you'd like to resign as my guide, I'll—"

"No, I'm sticking."

They rode in silence for a few minutes.

"My brother and I," she said finally, "used to have long debates on subjects like this. He always accused me of being too idealistic."

"What'd he think of your going into social work?"

"He never knew about that. He was already dead when I came over here."

"He must have died young."

"Yes, much too young."

The overhead speakers announced, "Knightsbridge Station. Final stop."

The tubetrain began slowing.

Marj said, "Let the other passengers get off first."

The car halted, the doors opened.

"Knightsbridge. All off."

When they were on the platform, Marj said quietly, "We want that door on the left, the one marked Staff Only."

"You visiting friends?"

"No, this is a shortcut over to the gang territory." She tapped on the metal door three times.

It slid open. Standing in the corridor beyond was a black-enameled robot wearing a stationmaster's cap. "Ah, a pleasure to see you, Miss Lofton, as always."

"I'm making a late call over there, Jarvis."

"This a beau of yours?"

"A colleague."

"Take good care of her, lad," the robot told him. "Were you to ask me, I'd say this is a very risky job she's got herself."

"I'll look after the lady," promised Jake. "Although she strikes me as being very capable on her own."

"Nobody's safe over there." Jarvis grunted and moved aside. "Good luck to both of you. I'm happy it's you who're making this little trip and not me."

Catching Jake's hand, Marj led him through another door and into a damp, dim-lit tunnel.

═25═

A SET OF portable earphones on his head, Gomez was roaming the living room of his hotel suite. "This Wexler *hombre* ought to be at Doc Danenberg's by now," he observed. "She phoned him nearly an hour ago."

"Investigative work, as you should've learned long since, requires considerable patience." Natalie was sitting in an armchair near one of the windows, holding her set of earphones in her lap. "I'd have thought, by the way, that a hotel of the stature of the Louvre provided maid service."

"That they do. A robot rolls in twice daily."

Glancing around, nose wrinkling, the reporter said, "Does that mean you managed to make all this mess just since the last cleaning?"

"There's no mess to be seen, *chiquita*."

"Well, probably you and I disagree as to

199

what constitutes a mess. To me two empty ale bottles lying on the sofa, a boot sprawled on the rug, and a pair of discarded undershorts dangling from a doorknob qualifies as a mess."

Gomez shook his head. "No, those are merely signs of a relaxed, low-pressure approach to life and— Bingo! Wexler has arrived."

"We'll continue this discussion of your slipshod habits later." She grabbed up her earphones.

"Why'd you allow him in?" the International Drug Agency Chief was asking the doctor.

"Bram, I've already explained that the man simply forced his way in here."

"He must be suspicious of you, Hilda. How did he—"

"I don't know how he knew I was in Paris. I called you to—"

"What did he say? Go over it again."

"A good deal of it was just babble and false amiability."

Natalie smiled. "She's certainly got you figured out."

"Silence, *por favor.*"

". . . anyway," Wexler was saying, "does he suspect your relationship with Kittridge?"

"He mentioned the professor. I don't know," said Dr. Danenberg. "Gomez and that damned partner of his obviously don't accept the idea that Bouchon was killed by the actual Unknown Soldier."

"Did he say why?"

"No, but it's clear they suspect a Tek link with the murder."

"It wasn't exactly a murder, Hilda. It was merely the elimination of a problem."

"The problem being that Bouchon became aware of what you're up to. You know, Bram, I can't help wondering if you perhaps haven't made someone else suspicious by your—"

"Bouchon was the only one we had to worry about."

"No, there's still Jake Cardigan to worry about. He seems to have some idea of what's really going on."

"So does this Gomez then."

"Yes, but Gomez is a halfwit, not a serious threat. I know Cardigan, though, and he—"

"Halfwit," echoed Natalie, nodding her head. "Another apt description."

"Hush up, *chiquita*." Gomez settled into a chair that put him with his back to her.

". . . and they don't know that Kittridge has managed to pass on to us, through you, a method for manufacturing a new SuperTek that will be immune to his chip-destroying system," Wexler said. "Nor do they have any idea where our new Teklab is located. So really there's no reason for—"

"Unless we stop him, Cardigan will find out."

"Cardigan is over in London, dear Hilda, and— Why are these dreadful flowers lying on the table?"

"Oh, that halfwit brought them and I haven't gotten around to disposing of them."

"Did you inspect them?"

"What do you mean?"

"Christ, Hilda! I mean he might've concealed an eavesdropping device in them."

"He's not bright enough for—"

"But he is. Here's a goddamn bug. Don't speak another word."

And they didn't.

In less than five minutes, probably using a portable bug detector, Wexler had discovered all the listening devices Gomez had planted during his recent visit to the doctor's place. All of them were speedily destroyed.

Yanking off his earphones, Gomez said, "Beth was right about distrusting her *padre.*" Standing up, he crossed to a window. "Super-Tek, huh? Those *cabrónes* never give up."

"I bet Bennett Sands is involved in this as well," said Natalie. "They got him out of prison to help on their new SuperTek project."

"*Sí,*" he agreed. "And Jake's ex-wife has to be mixed up in it, too."

Jake, led by Marj, emerged from the Underground and found himself in the ruins of a railway station. There were bodies scattered about, dozens of them, looking like bundles of rags and piles of discarded clothes.

"Lots of kids sleep here," explained Marj. "Especially the newcomers who haven't taken up with a gang yet."

It smelled hereabouts of sweat, decay, and illness. Jake noticed that one of the sleeping youths was hooked up to a battered Tek Brainbox.

As they worked their way through the sleepers toward the night street, Jake chanced to brush against the huddled figure of a thin girl.

The girl awakened, sat up, and screamed. *"Jesus! Jesus! Help!"*

"Easy, easy." Marj knelt beside her, putting an arm around her narrow shoulders. "It's okay, Sue."

The girl blinked, shook her head, came fully awake. "Oh, hi, Marj. What's wrong?"

"My friend accidently bumped into you. It must have tied in with a nightmare you were having."

"Yeah, I have a lot of nightmares." She hugged the older woman for a moment. "I hope I didn't scare anybody."

"Only me," Jake told her, grinning.

Letting go of her, Marj rose. "Take care, Sue."

"Best I can. 'Night." She settled down on the floor, readjusting her tattered coat around her.

Out on the street Marj said, "We never get

ahead. You help two kids get away from here and four new ones move in."

There was noise and light about a block away.

A caliope was playing Xmas carols, and lightsigns were flashing messages—SALVATION IS NOW!, IT'S NEVER TOO LATE TO MEND!, FREE MEALS 24 HOURS A DAY!, FATHER TIM'S MOBILE MISSION.

Marj nodded in the direction of the Mobile Mission. "We can talk to Father Tim first," she suggested. "He knows just about everything that's going on."

Father Tim was a plump jovial android dressed in a well-worn clerical suit. His mission was housed in a parked landvan that was festooned with lightsigns and speakers.

Inside the main cabin of the van was a small dining area where a tarnished robot was ladling out soup from a cauldron built into its chest. Three forlorn kids, the youngest about ten, were sitting at the table.

"Bless my soul—if I had one," said Father Tim, scratching at his curly white hair. "It does my old heart—if I had one of those either—good to see you, my child. And who's the pilgrim with you?"

While she shook hands with the android priest, Marj explained, "Father Tim, this is Jake Cardigan."

"The noted detective, is it?"

"The detective anyway." Jake shook hands with the mechanical man.

"Either of you folks care for a bowl of soup before we chat? Tonight it's Moonbase Gumbo."

Shaking her head, Marj said, "Jake is fairly certain his son, Dan, came over here a day or so ago. He was planning to contact somebody in the Westminsters."

"You've been away for a few days, my dear."

"Yes. Has something happened?"

"The TKs raided the hangout at the abbey," the priest informed her. "There was, I'm afraid, considerable killing."

Jake asked, "Do you know if my son was hurt?"

"I don't as yet have the names of any of the dead or injured," he replied. "But hear me out, the both of you. What happened next may have some bearing on your search. It seems the Tek Kids took some prisoners, along with considerable loot, back to their headquarters at the palace. That very night there was a ferocious raid on the TK enclave."

"By the Westminsters?" asked Marj.

"No, these were apparently outsiders. Mercenaries of some sort, I've been told," said Father Tim. "Came roaring in with considerable firepower and did a goodly amount of damage. The psi powers of the TKs didn't help them a bit. The raiders, in turn, took off with several prisoners. They also carried away the

205

Coronation Chair, which the Tek Kids had swiped during their raid at Westminster Abbey."

"You don't know the names of the kids who were taken?" asked Jake. "Or where they went?"

"I fear I do not," said the android. "Though if you can give me a day or so, I'm sure I can find out."

"We don't have a day," said Jake. "We've got to get some answers tonight."

—≡26≡—

THEY FOUND SILVERHAND Sally sitting on a pile
of rubble in one of the chapels of Westminster
Abbey. She had a leg folded under her and was
absently rubbing at the fine mist that was
forming on her metallic arm.

Marj said, "We'd like to talk with you,
Sally."

"All right," the girl replied in a faraway
voice.

"Something wrong?" She crouched beside
her.

"Oh, nothing special, Marj. When just about
everything is wrong, it's hard to pinpoint."

Jake told her, "I'm Jake Cardigan and—"

"I met your son."

"Is he here?"

"No," she replied, "not anymore."

"But he was?"

"Yes. Angel and Ludd brought him in. They

207

found him wandering around and brought him here."

"Do you know where Dan is now?"

Sally looked up at him. "I'm afraid maybe he did something really stupid," she said. "I warned him and so did Angel. He wouldn't listen."

Marj asked, "He came here searching for Nancy Sands, didn't he?"

"Sure, and when I told him the Tek Kids had taken her prisoner in a raid, well, he said he had to go over to the palace to find her." She rubbed again, slowly, at her arm. "I warned him that wasn't smart."

"Do you know for certain," Jake asked, "that he got there?"

"I'm pretty certain he did."

"Any idea what happened to him?"

"I don't think he's dead," said Sally. "Whoever it was that raided the TKs took some prisoners and maybe he was one of them."

"You sure of that?"

"All I know is that he wasn't among the dead ones. Neither was Nancy."

"We'll have to talk with the TKs," said Jake.

"Lancelot's dead," Sally informed him. "I don't know who the hell is running the gang now."

Jake sat down beside her. "You're a friend of Nancy's."

"Not a very good or reliable one, though.

After she came to me for help, she just got in deeper trouble."

"Why'd she come here?"

"She'd found out some things she didn't want to believe. Nancy thought of this as a sanctuary, a retreat where she could do some thinking. But, you know, Marj, that this really isn't a good place for anybody."

"What had she found out that upset her so?" asked Marj.

"Nancy didn't tell me everything, but I know it had to do with her father."

"With his escape from prison?"

"Did he escape? I didn't know that," said Sally. "But, yeah, that must be part of it. I think she found out that somebody high up in the Tek trade was financing a breakout. She hadn't, you know, allowed herself to suspect her dad was tied in with the Tek cartels."

Jake patted her on the shoulder. "Thanks for your help," he said, standing.

"I don't think I've been much help to you," said Sally. "Nor to anybody else."

"It was Nancy's decision to come here," reminded Marj. "And Dan made up his own mind to follow her."

"We'd best head over to the palace," suggested Jake.

Sally touched Marj's arm with her real fingers. "Maybe," she said quietly, "sometime soon we can talk about my getting out of here."

Marj smiled. "That's a good idea."

"The thing is," said Sally forlornly, "I don't want to stay here—and I can't go home."

Bundled up in his new thermocoat, Gomez made his solo way along the late-night Avenue Victor Hugo. He was striding briskly, to prevent his blood from turning to ice in his veins. The night was bleak and bitterly cold.

When the chilled detective tried to whistle a seasonal tune, his breath came out as wispy mist.

"Remind me," he said to himself, "to spend next Xmas someplace in the tropics."

The robot doorman in front of the Hôtel Hernani had apparently frozen earlier in the evening. Two uniformed bellbots were pouring steaming hot water over him from silver teapots.

Three doors past the hotel was the Kowboy Kitchen. It offered, according to the lightsign pulsing in its window, AUTHENTIC AMERICAN CHOW!

Shivering once, Gomez pushed through the swinging doors.

The simulated scents of frying meat and simmering onions and potatoes hit him as he crossed the small foyer.

"Howdy, pard!" greeted a huge bronzed robot decked out in a passable approximation of early twentieth-century cowboy garb. "Welcome to our homey little chuckwagon."

"Well, sir, that's right neighborly of you." Gomez was looking beyond the robot and into the small dining room.

There were only five customers scattered around at the small tables. Alone at the table next to the potted artificial cactus was the man he'd come to see.

"You want a table all by your lonesome?" inquired the jovial robot. "Or are you—"

"I'll be joining a friend yonder," replied the detective. "I'll just mosey over to his table."

The small Chinese was hunched slightly in his chair, frowning at the dozen watches built into his cyborg right arm. "Shit, Gomez, you're eight minutes and fifteen seconds late."

Sitting down, Gomez said, "That's because I froze twice en route and had to wait until some good samaritans poured boiling water over me."

"Don't you carry a watch?"

"When you reach my advanced years, Time-check, you don't want to be reminded of the swift, inexorable rushing passage of time."

"You've always had a negative view of temporal matters, daddy," said Timecheck. "I'll tell you something. Since I've relocated in Paris from Kyoto, Japan, I've found the folks here to be very much obsessed with time. It's, hey, a real gasseroo to be doing business in a nation of clock watchers instead of a lot of Zen types."

211

"Speaking of business, what have you found out for me?"

Timecheck was scowling at another of his built-in timepieces. "Berkeley, California, is six secs slow again. That's a pisser, because now I'm going to have to—"

"Information," reminded Gomez.

"Aren't you going to join me for a snack?"

"Nope."

"You really ought to have a fixed schedule for your meals, daddy. Myself, I always have a midnight snack between 11:58 P.M. and 12:32 A.M. That way, no matter where I might happen to—"

"Excalibur," said Gomez quietly.

Timecheck brought his metal arm up to his ear, listened to several of his watches in turn. "I don't like the sound of Cairo time."

"Electronic watches don't make any noise."

"Sure, they do." He lowered his arm, then tugged at his ear with the fingers of his real hand. "You just got to know how to listen."

"I am prepared to listen," Gomez informed him, "to any and all scuttlebutt for which the Cosmos Detective Agency is paying you a ridiculous and overblown fee."

The young Chinese rolled down his jacket sleeve, covering most of the watch faces. "So far I've been able to establish that this guy Wexler is a dyed-in-the-wool member of the Excalibur outfit." He picked up his chili soyburger and took a bite. "You really ought to try the chow here."

"Back to Wexler."

"He's a big man in Excalibur. Those gonzos want a king to rule Merrie Old England once again," said the informant. "Toppling the established democratic government of Great Britain takes dough. How are these jerkoffs going to raise the bucks? The answer, my friend, is—"

"By peddling Tek."

"Yowsah, you got it. Rumor has it there's something called SuperTek about to hit the market. This new stuff is more powerful than regular Tek and it's designed to withstand any destructive devices turned against it," said Timecheck, taking another bite of the burger. "SuperTek sounds like a neat idea to me, Gomez, and if these ginks were selling stock, I'd buy a sizable—"

"What about Dr. Danenberg?"

"The old bimbo's a buddy of Wexler."

"That I know."

"But she's not a card-carrying member of Excalibur. The skirt doesn't care if King Arthur II sits on the throne or on a portable biffy." He paused, rubbing his thumb and forefinger together. "The good doctor is in it strictly for the old cumshaw."

Nodding, Gomez asked, "You got anything on her itinerary?"

"She's departing Paris comes the dawn tomorrow."

"Bound for where?"

"London."

"London," said Gomez. "It's not likely to be any warmer than Paris. But I've got a feeling I'd better follow her there."

Morgana was leaning against the base of the Queen Victoria Memorial, arms folded across her narrow chest. "You missed all the excitement, Marj," she said. "Who's your friend? He's carrying one of those damn scramblers of yours and I can't get at his mind."

"I'm Jake Cardigan. Did my son—"

"Dan? Yes, he was here," she answered. "I do hope he's not going to end up looking as world-weary and shopworn as you do, love. He's a handsome lad, he is."

Marj asked her, "What happened to him?"

Shrugging her left shoulder, Morgana answered, "The bastards carried him off, along with that Nancy bitch."

"Who were they?" asked Jake.

She shrugged both shoulders. "They were all equipped with blockers. I couldn't read a single thought," she said. "Hired hands, my guess would be, outsiders and not kids. Old sods some of them, in their forties and more."

"How many were there?"

"At least two dozen. They used landcars,

skycars, and a stewpot of weapons. It was fast and efficient and a lot of us got killed."

"Any of them killed?"

"Only two or three."

"Where are the bodies?"

She cocked a thumb in the direction of the ruined palace. "We dumped them out in front. For the dogs and rats to eat."

Jake walked in the direction Morgana had indicated.

Marj followed him.

There were three bodies, two men and a woman, laid out side by side on the rutted ground.

Kneeling, Jake started to search one of the men. After a moment he stood. "Nothing on him, no ID packet."

Frowning, Marj moved over to look down at the dead woman. "I know this one," she told him. "A longtime raider for hire."

"Know whom she worked for?"

"Yes, I know who probably provided her and the others," answered Marj. "We ought to be able to persuade him to tell us who the mercenaries were working for and where they took Dan and Nancy."

Morgana drifted over to them. "I have a feeling," she said, "that we've maybe been sold out."

Jake asked, "How so?"

"We're very much for monarchy, for the old times when the first King Arthur ruled and

England was a decent, well-ordered place to live," she explained. "Hell, we took our bloody names, a lot of us, from the old stories about him and his knights."

"Who betrayed you?"

"I'm not certain, but those bastard raiders took the Coronation Chair. Seems to me they have some use for it in mind," Morgana said. "If they'd told us what they were planning, that they were monarchists, too, why, we might have given it to them and there wouldn't have been any damn killing at all."

"They probably do have a use for the throne," agreed Jake. "But they wanted Nancy Sands, too. She's important enough to them that they'll kill to get hold of her."

"And what makes that bitch so special?"

Jake said, "I don't have a complete answer yet."

══27══

THE NEW VAUXHALL Mall rose up twenty stories beside a safe stretch of the Thames. The seethrough elevator carried Jake and Marj up past the bright-lit twenty-four-hour shops and restaurants toward the quieter commercial tiers.

"Is this Edwin Bozwell likely to be here this late?" asked Jake as they rose slowly upward.

"Far as I know, Bozwell just about lives in his offices."

"What business does he pretend to be in?"

"He calls himself a theatrical agent," she replied. "He does book an occasional act, mostly mechanical stuff. Andy strippers, roboxers, programmed puppets and the like."

"But his real vocation is providing sluggers and stormtroopers?"

Nodding, Marj said, "Nobody's been able to prove it, but Bozwell's the major supplier of mercenaries in England."

"The dead girl was one of his, huh?"

"Yes, another runaway who graduated to better things."

The elevator halted at Level 37, the doors moved aside.

The office they sought had an opaque plasti-glass door with BOZWELL TALENT AGENCY etched on it in gilt.

Marj tapped the door and it slid open.

The office was small and cluttered, reeking of spicy food and machine oil. Bozwell himself, a puffy dark man of thirty-five, was sitting behind a small neowood desk and eating something green out of a plazcarton with a pair of thin metallic chopsticks. All around him rose stacks of old-fashioned costume trunks, storage bins, massive packing crates, and spills and tangles of spangled clothes.

"Marjie, Marjie," he said in his croaking voice. "It's a frigging pleasure to see you once again. Who's the john?"

Smiling, Marj pushed aside a pile that was a mix of faxscripts and vidcassettes. "You're losing weight, Edwin." She perched on the desk edge.

Carefully, Bozwell sealed the carton and set it aside. Then he wiped the chopsticks, thoroughly, on a plyochief and returned them to their neoleather case. "Actually, Marjie honey, I'm down almost eleven ounces this past week alone. So who did you say this guy is?"

"A friend," she said.

"That's nice you got a few frigging friends," the fat agent said. "Being a loner, let me tell you, can drive you bughouse."

"Guess who I just saw over on the gangside, Edwin?"

"I haven't the faintest frigging idea."

"Annie Kettleman."

"That name doesn't ring a single chime with me, Marjie honey."

Marj leaned closer to him. "Annie worked for you."

"Nope, wrong. I don't represent any talent named Annie Kellerman."

"Annie Kettleman—and, sure, you do," she said. "She's been a mercenary on your list for over a year. I know, because I've been trying to persuade her to quit for almost that long."

"C'mon, Marjie," complained Bozwell, annoyed. "You're babbling like a frigging bobby. I am, pure and simple, a theatrical agent. I know, yeah, there have been dirty rumors circulating that I book mercenaries, killers, and all sorts of unsavory types." He reached for the chopstick case. "It's been truly swell seeing you again, but now, honey, I got other—"

"Edwin, I can be, as you know, awfully nasty," she reminded him as, smiling, she took hold of his coat collar. "And my friend here— he's even worse. So what say you tell us all about who contracted for two dozen or so of your prize mercenaries to raid the Tek Kids' hideout?"

"I don't know a frigging thing about—"

"Edwin, I wish you'd be serious." Swinging out with her right hand, she slapped the fat man hard across the face.

He glared up at her. "Good thing you're a dame, honey," he said in his croaking voice. "Otherwise, it'd be your bum in a sling about now."

She slapped him again, even harder. "I know damn well you sent Annie over there to get killed," she said. "Tell me who—"

"All I've got to tell you is to get the hell out of my frigging office." Bozwell got suddenly to his feet, making a sweeping movement with his left arm that knocked Marj off the desk and against a tower of cartons. Stumbling, her ankle turned under her and she fell to the floor. She landed on her side and cried out in pain.

Jake was reaching for his stungun.

Behind the angry agent a panel in the opaque office wall whipped open.

Two large and formidable androids came charging into the room.

Dan had awakened with the sun shining brightly in his face.

He was sitting in a high-backed wicker chair, slumped against a collection of colorful pillows. The high, wide window a few feet in front of him showed a stretch of empty yellow beach. Beyond that was nothing but intensely blue water.

A lone gull came swooping down through the bright, clear afternoon sky. It made a slow, lazy circle close to the surface of the sea. All at once its left wing fell off its body.

The gull, wobbling, tried to climb higher. Instead, though, it fell, hitting the surface with a splash and swiftly sinking.

"That's the third one today," said someone behind him. "They're obviously not buying top-of-the-line botbirds."

"Nancy!" Dan started to get up, but neither of his legs went along with the idea. Feeling suddenly dizzy, he sank into the chair. It creaked loudly.

The girl, who'd been standing just behind his chair, moved up to take hold of his hand. "They used a stungun on you, Dan," she told him. "You'd better take it easy for a while."

"Let me ask a few questions." He held on tightly to her hand.

She rested one hip against the arm of the chair. "Go ahead, but don't try to get up and walk around just yet."

"I remember coming to after that asshole— Excuse me, after Merlin used his telek abilities on me and knocked me out."

"I met Merlin. He was an asshole."

"Okay, then I woke up inside Buckingham

Palace. You were there, and that guy named Lancelot."

"Yes. When I heard you'd been captured, I insisted that Lancelot let me see you."

"Did he . . . I mean, they told me that he—"

"We can talk about that later."

Dan looked up at her face. "Right after you got there, almost one whole wall of the room we were in seemed to explode away and—" He shook his head slowly. "That's about all I can remember, Nancy. Except that a couple of big guys in black suits started to grab you."

"When you tried to stop them, one of them used his stungun on you."

"And they brought us here?"

She nodded. "They killed quite a few of the others."

"Why'd they spare us?"

"Me they spared because of my father," she explained. "You they brought along because they're not sure how much I may've confided in you. And they're curious about what you may have told to somebody else."

"Where the hell are we exactly?"

"We're up in an orbiting resort satellite," she answered. "It's a place called the Caribbean Colony. Very exclusive and expensive, despite the defective gulls."

"Obviously, huh, it's more than just a resort?"

"They've got a very efficient Teklab hidden away in the innards of this thing."

"Okay, now tell me who they are—some of the big Tek cartels?"

Letting go of his hand, she walked closer to the window. "I'd better explain why I ran away," she said, watching the bright simulated afternoon. "I overheard the McCays talking."

"I know. You hinted to me that you'd learned things about them."

"I didn't want to tell you everything back then," she said. "Mostly because I didn't want to believe what was really going on. Instead, I ran away, planning to spend a few days with Sally. I had the childish idea that I'd be able to get everything sorted out."

"This has to do with your father, doesn't it?"

"Oh, yes, it does. Very much to do with Bennett Sands, noted industrialist and jailbird." She turned to face him again. "He's right here in the satellite with us. I haven't seen him yet, but—"

"Hey, wait. The last time I heard, he was in that maxsec prison near Bunter Academy."

"He escaped, with a lot of outside help," she said. "That happened while you were hunting for me."

"The escape—that's one of the things you heard them talking about, isn't it?"

"One of the things," she admitted quietly.

"Why is he here?"

"Well, my father is practically running this

whole damned operation." Very quietly, the girl began to cry.

This time Dan was able to stand. He made it to Nancy's side and put an arm around her. "It's okay," he assured her. "We're together now and—"

"No, Dan, nothing is okay, nothing at all," she said. "Go back and sit down. I'm going to have to try to tell you as much as I know and—hell, I'm sorry, but some of it isn't going to be very pleasant for you to hear."

William Shatner

$\equiv$ **28** $\equiv$

THE LARGE BLOND android sprinted, hopped atop Bozwell's desk, and then came hurtling at Jake.

Jake meantime bicycled backwards, drew his stungun, and dropped to the floor.

The heavy mechanical man sailed clean over him to slam into a costume trunk.

The lid of the trunk popped open; bright crimson and gold plumes and swirls of silvery ribbon came spewing out to shower the android.

Bounding upright, Jake fired at him.

The blond andy snarled, made an attempt to catch hold of Jake. But he suddenly stiffened, disabled. He gave out a series of staccato gagging noises, falling over sideways. He toppled a stack of cartons and they came falling down all around him as he smacked out flat on the office floor.

Turning, Jake saw that the other android was kneeling over the fallen Marj, wide legs straddling her. He was using both of his powerful hands to choke her.

Not hesitating, Jake aimed his stungun and fired again.

The large android jerked to an upright position, hands leaving the woman's throat. His arms went back, elbows jabbing at the air. He ceased to function, dropping over with a thud.

"I'm warning you," shouted Bozwell, who was huddled behind his desk, gripping a lazgun in both fat hands. "Get your arse out of my office."

Jake kicked out suddenly, sending the desk slamming back into the agent. Bozwell was shoved against the wall, his gunhand hit against a panel and he let go of his weapon.

Lunging, Jake grabbed him and dumped him down into his chair. "Stay there," he suggested.

He backed up, eyes on Bozwell, and crouched beside Marj. "You okay?"

In a thin, raw voice she managed to reply, "More or less."

Nodding, Jake snatched up the fallen lazgun. He thrust his own stungun away and walked close to the seated Bozwell. "Where's my son?"

"I don't even know your frigging name, let alone the current whereabouts of your—"

"I'm Jake Cardigan. My son's name is Dan."

He swung the lazgun up and poked it hard into the fat man's middle. "I want to know where Dan and Nancy Sands were taken."

"I never heard of her either. So you—"

"Look at me," requested Jake in a level voice. "I ran out of patience about ten minutes ago. Tell me where my son is."

"All right, all right." The agent was sweating, running his tongue over his upper lip. "You don't have to act like a frigging maniac."

"Who hired your mercenaries?"

"Outfit calls itself Excalibur."

"What were your instructions?"

"To get Nancy Sands and your boy away from the Tek Kids," answered Bozwell. "Anybody who stood in the way, we should kill."

"How'd they know Nancy was at Buckingham Palace?"

"They had people hunting for the girl since she ran off. Somebody figured Danny might lead them to her, so they put a tail on him. They followed the kid and he did lead them to her."

Jake asked, "Where are they now?"

"I'm not exactly sure."

He poked the gun barrel deeper. "Make a good guess."

"Up in the Caribbean Colony satellite," answered the perspiring fat man. "The Excalibur bunch, they have a hideout there. I also hear maybe Bennett Sands is lying low at the Colony, too. That's where your kid must be."

Jake placed the lazgun on the desk. He drew out his stungun. "Thanks for your help." He squeezed the trigger and Bozwell slumped into a coma that would last for a full day or more.

"We'll have to get up to that satellite as soon as we can," he said, turning back to Marj.

She was standing, leaning against a heavy trunk, but her face was pale. "Maybe you'll have to make that trip without me," she said, rubbing at the red welts on her throat. "I feel—"

Her eyes drifted shut and she fell forward into Jake's arms.

Marj lived in a cottage in Maida Vale. Her bedroom had a one-way plastiglass wall that gave a view of the small, night-filled garden outside.

She was sitting up on her circular bed. "I'm fine now, really," she assured Jake. "And, listen—I'm sorry, Jake, that I sidetracked you."

Jake occupied a lucite chair near the bed. "All part of the courteous Cosmos service," he told her, grinning. "We always see ailing social workers safely home—especially after they've been wrestling with androids."

She smiled, touching her fingertips to her throat. "I know you must want to get up to the Caribbean Colony right away."

"Sure, but I couldn't have left you lying around on Bozwell's office floor."

"Are you going to tell Scotland Yard that Bennett Sands is probably up there?"

"Eventually," he answered. "First, though, I have to get Dan safely away from there."

"You're planning to hit the Colony alone?"

Jake nodded. "I want to look around before I make a move. I figure I ought to be able to pass for a tourist."

"For a while anyway," she said. "There are several resort hotels there, three or four large casinos, and a great many simulated beaches. Hundreds of tourists go there every day."

"Seems likely that some of the major Teklords must control the place."

"Yes, that's near certain. Since they aren't especially fond of you, and since Sands doesn't much care for you either, Jake, you're going to have to be damn careful once you get there."

"Soon as you're feeling better, I'll head over to the London Spaceport and unobtrusively book passage on the earliest shuttle for the Caribbean Colony."

"Oh, I'm perfectly well right now." Marj edged off the bed and stood. "In fact, I don't know why I fainted at all."

Leaving his chair, he moved to her side. "Better sit down."

"No, I . . ." She hesitated, frowning. Then, reaching out, she took hold of him. "That's . . . funny."

"What's wrong, Marj?"

"I suddenly feel very unsteady," she told him

229

in a weak voice. "I saw some zigzags of colored light, too."

He guided her back to her bed, set her on it, and then sat close beside her. "Let me phone a medic to—"

"No, there's no need for a doctor, really." She put her arms around him, resting her cheek against his chest. "I hate to admit this, since I'm somebody who braves the worst gang areas of London, but tonight I'm feeling frightened."

Jake gently stroked her back. "Everybody feels like that sometimes."

"You too?"

"Sure."

Raising her head, she looked into his eyes. Then, leaning, she kissed him. After a moment she asked, "Could you . . . stay with me tonight?"

"Guess I'd better," he said quietly.

—≡29≡—

GOMEZ DECIDED AGAINST whistling.

He kept his mouth tightly shut as he stepped from the warm lobby of the Louvre Hotel and into the bitterly cold dawn street. A light snow was falling straight down through the frigid morning.

"There's a most strange smell in the air, monsieur," observed the chef, who was filling in as bellbot and carrying Gomez's single suitcase.

"My coat."

The chef glanced over at him. "Ah, *oui*. So it is. The garment appears to be smoldering."

"Does that at highest setting."

"Next time you purchase a thermocoat in Paris, monsieur, ask me first. I can send you to a shop where you'll get— But here comes your landcab."

A maroon vehicle was pulling up at the curb.

When it halted, a chrome-plated robot in a long tan overcoat stepped out. "You order the Vite Cab?"

"Yeah," admitted Gomez.

The chef stepped forward to turn Gomez's suitcase over to the cabbie for stowing. His foot hit a patch of snow-covered ice and he went sliding uncontrollably ahead.

His cap fell off and he stumbled into the robot driver. The suitcase swung up, slamming the cabbie in the groin.

"Yow," yelled the robot, hopping back, bumping into his parked cab, bringing both hands up to his crotch.

"Robots don't have balls," realized Gomez. He sent a hand burrowing into his thermocoat and yanked out his stungun.

The spurious robot was turning toward him, one hand abandoning his crotch to slip into an overcoat pocket for a gun.

Gomez fired.

The beam of the stungun took the driver in the left ribs. He gasped, staggered, and fell. His metal head popped off as he hit the paving, revealing the face of a Parisian goon beneath it.

"Something's very much amiss," commented the chef as he struggled to get up.

"*Sí*," agreed Gomez.

From down the dawn street two other louts were running.

Pausing only to grab his suitcase, Gomez jumped into the driveseat of the landcab.

Doors flapping, he drove it away down the snowy thoroughfare.

Jake awakened suddenly.

The night was gone and gray daybreak was showing at the one-way plastiglass wall of the bedroom.

Yawning once, he turned to look at Marj.

She was no longer there beside him.

He reached over, touching the place where she'd been lying. It was cold.

Jake sat up, glancing around the room.

Then he became aware of a faint murmuring. It sounded like two people in conversation somewhere in the cottage.

Very quietly Jake left the bed. He walked to the partially open doorway. One of the voices was Marj's, the other was that of a young man. Jake couldn't make out any actual words.

They sounded as though they were in the kitchen.

Slowly and silently, Jake dressed. When he picked up his shoulder holster to strap it on, he discovered that his stungun was missing.

He took time to search the bedroom for it, even though he didn't expect to find the weapon there.

Easing out into the early morning hallway, Jake stood listening.

The murmured conversation was still going on. The young man sounded angry.

Jake walked to the kitchen and pushed the door open.

The yellow room was empty.

But he could still hear the voices.

He crossed to the open pantry door and looked in. At the back of it a wide panel stood open.

". . . and the best news is, after all, that you'll be able to kill Bennett Sands," Marj was saying.

"That's great, but did you have to sleep with that damned cop to find out?"

"Listen, nothing happened . . . really. But I did have to get close to him," she answered. "I knew he'd probably find out where Sands was hiding—and he did."

"Hell, you could've located Bennett without the help of some over-the-hill gumshoe," said the young man. "You found all the others for me."

Moving to the opening, Jake looked in.

A short ramp led down to a brightly lit electronics laboratory. Marj, wearing a lab coat, was perched on one of the workbenches. Leaning against the opposite bench was a young man with a bushy moustache. His hair was short-cropped and he wore an earring made of a Brazilian coin.

"The important thing is that we've located

Sands," Marj persisted. "Now you have to get up to the Caribbean Colony and—"

"Good morning." Jake entered the lab.

"Hello, Jake, I figured you'd find your way down here sooner or later," said Marj, smiling. "I'd like you to meet my brother."

Singing enthusiastically and banging on a drum, Gomez entered the Central Paris Subtrain Depot. He was clad in a long dark overcoat, a pulled-down cap, and a muffler that covered a good portion of his face. Two caroling androids, similarly attired, were marching in front of him and three followed behind.

The group halted on the platform for the Paris-London tunnel train. The first android, after adjusting his cap, set up a large glosign that proclaimed they were collecting funds for the International Salvation Army.

Gomez, as he whapped the drum, scanned the figures that were scattered along the platform. Passengers were boarding the compartment cars, friends, some of them yawning drowsily, were seeing them off.

Standing over near a lopsided soycaf kiosk was Timecheck. He was nibbling a croissant while consulting several of his built-in watches.

Gomez, moving away from his fellow carolers, sidled over to the young Chinese. "Spare a few francs for a worthy cause?" he inquired, holding out his palm.

"Do a swift scramola, buddy," advised the informant.

"I'm glad my disguise is foolproof." Gomez set down the drum. "Pretend to be forking over a charitable contribution."

"Shit, Gomez, you're seven minutes and thirteen seconds late."

"Is Dr. Danenberg on board the train?"

"Yeah, the quiff got here, alone, twelve minutes ago." Rolling down his sleeve, Timecheck began pretending to search his pockets. "Always glad to help a wonderful organization like yours, chum," he said in a louder voice.

"That didn't ring especially sincere. No matter." Gomez looked around. "Have you spotted any goons or louts hereabouts?"

Timecheck shook his head. "Just the usual grifters, pimps, pickpockets, teleks, and con artists. Why?"

"Somebody tried to do me serious harm as I was departing my hotel."

"You figure Dr. Danenberg arranged that?"

"She or her associates, *sí.*"

"Well, I haven't seen any unusual thugs since I arrived here thirteen minutes and eight—make that nine seconds ago."

Gomez nodded toward the waiting train. "What compartment is Dr. D. in?"

"Twenty-six C—two cars up."

"I'm wondering if my already booked compartment is going to prove safe."

"As I say, I haven't noticed any pro killers

hanging around. But, you know, to be on the safe side, maybe you should bunk with the other skirt.''

Gomez frowned. ''What lady are you alluding to?''

''That reporter bimbo.''

''Natalie? Is Natalie Dent aboard this self-same train?''

''She climbed aboard nine minutes and seventeen seconds ago.''

''She alone?''

''Far as I could tell.''

''I was hoping I'd ditched her.''

''She's a smart cookie. That time I met her in Kyoto, she struck me as—''

''I'd best hop on the train,'' said Gomez. ''What room is Nat occupying?''

''Forty-two B—four cars up.''

''Return, *por favor,* the drum to my musical colleagues.''

''It's heavy.''

''Bill me for the chore.''

''Okay. You only got one minute and twenty-three seconds before the train pulls out. You better hurry.''

Hurrying, Gomez entered the Paris-London Subtrain.

He stood in the corridor, trying to decide which compartment to go to.

—=30=—

"YOUR BROTHER, HUH?" Jake took a few more steps across the laboratory floor. "I thought he was dead."

"Do I look dead, asshole?" asked Richard Lofton.

"Richard, please," said Marj in a gentle voice. "You go sit in your favorite chair while Jake and I talk."

"Sis, I'm not a goddamn kid. You don't have to treat me like—"

"Darling, please."

"Okay, but there's no need to nag my butt off." Shoulders hunched, he shuffled to a high-back wicker chair and dropped into it.

Jake said to the young woman, "So you didn't give up robotics?"

"I started working on him nearly two years ago," she said, one leg swinging back and forth as she sat on the edge of the lab table. "In my spare time, originally just to take my mind off all the dreadful stuff I was running into working for the Welfare Squad."

"How close a sim is he?"

"Oh, he's Richard," she answered. "Richard, that is, as he was just before he died. Well, no. Actually, he's spruced up a bit, since he was in pretty bad shape by then."

"Hey, I'm sitting right here in the same goddamn room," reminded the android. "I'm hearing all this, you know."

"Yes, but you needn't be upset," she told the replica of her dead brother. "Richard was in his early twenties when he was killed. He'll always be in his early twenties."

Jake leaned against the lab table that faced hers. "Killed in a Brazil War?"

"Richard fought in the last one, but he survived."

"Survived? Survived, my ass," said her brother. "I was screwed up beyond recognition by that damn war. Shit, I turned into a Tekhead. It wasn't my fault, lots of guys tried Tek down there. You could just hook up to your Brainbox and pretend the fucking war had never happened."

"No one is criticizing you, dear," she assured him. "After a while, needing money badly and not wanting to borrow from me, he—"

"I did try to borrow from you, sis, and you

cut me off. You told me, 'No more dough for Tek dreams.' "

"I think you misunderstood what I was trying to—"

"Sure, I misunderstood. That's why I took a job with Bennett and worked at one of his rural Tek factories in Brasilia."

Marj said, "Bennett Sands . . ." She paused, shaking her head. "He somehow got the idea that my brother intended to double-cross him by selling information to a rival cartel."

"That guy's a real bastard," added Richard. "He didn't even, you know, give me a chance to explain. Had five of his thugs—and it took five to handle me—had them drag my poor ass out into the jungle and kill me. You know how they did it?"

"Dear, you needn't upset yourself by discussing—"

"It doesn't bother me now. Those greaseballs cut me into pieces with lazguns," explained her brother. "Sliced me into quarters. My guts spilled out all over the ground and you should've seen the fucking insects and animals that came out to feed on me."

"That's enough, Richard."

He folded his arms, shut his eyes, and leaned back in the creaking chair.

Marj said, "I got the notion—oh, several months ago, this was—that it would be fun to use this replica of Richard to kill Bennett Sands."

"Sounds like fun, yeah."

"But, Jake," she said, smiling at him, "mostly because of you, Sands was arrested and stuck away in a maximum security prison in NorCal. I couldn't think of any way to get at him."

"Is that when you decided to kill the others?"

"Actually, Jake, I'd made up a tentative list even before I started working on Richard," she told him. "Sands' name obviously led all the rest. When I realized, however, that he might well be permanently unavailable, we decided to go after the rest of them."

"How," inquired Jake, "did they earn a position on your list?"

"Richard and I decided to kill everyone responsible for his death."

"That was just Bennett Sands," said Jake, "and his hired hands, wasn't it?"

"If I hadn't been talked into joining the damn army," explained Richard, "if those political bastards hadn't lied about what was really going on down there—"

"Don't make yourself uneasy, Richard. I can tell him."

"And the fucking Teklords. Got me hooked, then some of them set me up and made it look as though I'd screwed Bennett."

Jake asked her, "How many names are on your list?"

"We have a few more to cross off yet." She smiled faintly.

"But Bouchon wasn't one of your targets?"

"Those assholes, whoever they are," complained Richard, "are trying to set me up again."

"Three of the killings, including the murder of your client's husband, were poor imitations of the Unknown Soldier's methods and style," Marj said. "I'm really surprised that the international police authorities have been taken in."

Jake boosted himself up, sitting on the edge of his lab table. "You got to know me because I might lead you to Sands."

"Ever since I heard he'd been transferred to England, I'd been keeping close track of him," she replied. "Then, when Beth phoned and suggested that I help you out—well, that seemed an enormous piece of luck for us. I realized you'd probably be crossing paths with him, since you were tracking down his missing daughter. Yes, I'm afraid that's why I volunteered to be your guide."

"And why we slept together."

"That's a bit more complicated," she said. "But basically I wanted to decoy you here."

"That whole business was stupid," put in her brother. "You didn't need him to find Bennett for us. Christ, we always find them, just the two of us. We never needed help from outside the family or—"

243

"We don't agree on this, Richard, but there's no reason to argue. Especially in front of company."

Jake said, "Marj, I'm going to make a pretty obvious comment now. Something, I'm certain, you must've thought about while—"

"I'm not insane," she assured him. "And, yes, I have considered the possibility. Very thoroughly."

"Building a machine to kill people, sending it out to check victims off a list," he said, "isn't exactly something a—"

"Jake, it's done all the time," she pointed out. "Your Teklord friends, for instance, use kamikaze androids. Many governments, including our own here in England, have several projects in the works that—"

"Be that as it may, you have to stop."

"I'm afraid I can't. Not until Richard and I have finished what we agreed to do."

"Richard didn't agree to anything," Jake said evenly. "He's been dead for years."

"I told you, sis, this guy isn't worth talking to."

"Suppose you phone Beth," suggested Jake. "Talk to her about this. She's a friend of yours and—"

"Jake, I don't need any advice, nor even a shoulder to cry on." Marj slipped her right hand into a pocket of her smock. "We intend to take care of Bennett Sands."

Jake said, "I'll take care of him."

"You'll just turn him over to the law," said Richard, leaving his chair. "They'll put him back into another fancy lockup."

"It's very important that Sands, as did the others, die in a certain way," she told Jake. "He has to see Richard before he's killed and realize who he is. That's the whole point."

"Marj, this whole—"

"I borrowed your stungun, Jake." She produced it from her pocket.

"Before you—"

She shot him.

=31=

NATALIE DENT, ARMS folded, knees pressed tight together, was glowering across her train compartment at Gomez. "Several years ago, when I was somewhat more innocent and naive than at present," she was saying to the curly-haired detective, "I, being, as I say, naive and innocent, brought home a stray mutt. He was a pathetic, sickly creature and the look in his dim, watery little eyes was very much like the sappy expression you assume whenever you're trying to wheedle and cajole some out-rageous favor out of me or—"

"Halt the flow of autobiography for a sec, *princesa*." He was using her vidphone.

The reporter's nose wrinkled. "The moral of this particular anecdote is—"

"Hush up, *por favor*."

A gleaming, ballheaded robot had reap-peared on the phonescreen. "I'm sorry, sir," it told him, "but Mr. Cardigan is not in his room here at the Crystal Palace Hotel. Nor has he left any message for a Mr. Pollino."

"Okay, *gracias.*"

"Your name isn't Pollino," mentioned Natalie.

"It's simply one of the code names that Jake and I use when—"

"Little-boy stuff," observed Natalie, unfolding her arms, scratching the tip of her faintly freckled nose, and refolding her arms.

"Have I told you, *florita,* how much I appreciate your allowing me to enjoy the sanctuary of your quarters whilst we wend our underwater way to London?"

"Sanctuary, at least as it's most frequently defined in most of the civilized sections of the globe, rarely includes phone privileges," she pointed out. "On top of which, Gomez, you ate most of my breakfast."

"That's what teamwork is all about, Nat," he informed her. "Sharing."

"You mean the way you shared your information on what Dr. Danenberg was up to?"

"But you did, as I well knew you would, get on the doctor's trail. And fate, which seems to be looking after us, did indeed bring us together once more." He held up his hand in a stop-now gesture. "A couple more quick calls, *chiquita,* and I should have all sorts of new info to share with you."

"He messed on my thermorug, too, causing

the darn thing to short-circuit," she said. "Then he bit my ankle."

"Whom are we discussing?"

"That stray puppy I was telling you about, Gomez, the one I foolishly took in out of a rainstorm," she answered. "He looked, especially around the eyes, a great deal like you."

"Well, the misguided attribution of human qualities to the lower animals can screw you up." He punched out another number on her vidphone.

The screen remained dark, but a raspy voice said, "London's fashionable Hotel Marryat. Yeah?"

"Mrs. Humphry Ward, if you please."

"Who's calling?"

"Tell her Sid."

Natalie unfolded her arms and crossed her legs. "That's a dippy name—Mrs. Humphry Ward."

"An alias."

"Gomez, my love, how the bloody hell are you?" inquired a throaty woman's voice. The screen was still blank.

"Muy bien, Mrs. W. And you?"

"Can't complain, Sid. How may I be of assistance?"

Gomez nodded at the screen. "A Dr. Hilda Danenberg is, as we speak, en route to your fair city," he explained. "See if you can find out what she's planning to do over the next day or so. The lady's linked with a few Tek cartels, I believe, and with the Excalibur Movement."

"Those loons."

"I'll contact you after I arrive in London."

"You're coming here, too, my love?"

"I am, *sí.*"

"We'll have to hoist a few."

"If time permits, *bonita*. We're paying the usual fee, by the way. *Adiós.*"

"He ate my canary, too," said Natalie.

"Stray dogs will do that," said Gomez, making another call.

London was slightly warmer than Paris. Gomez was able to turn his thermocoat down a notch and that kept it from smoldering.

Alone now, though obligated to join Natalie for tea that afternoon, he was roaming the city. His concern was growing since he hadn't been able as yet to find any trace of Jake.

Gomez had just called on Arthur Bairnhouse at the Hewitt Inquiry Agency and was experiencing mixed feelings. The operative he'd arranged for when he'd phoned from the tubetrain had picked up Dr. Danenberg's trail at the London station and followed her to the flat she was using near Regent's Park. It was gratifying to know where she was at the moment, but he was also anxious to locate his partner.

The pink-faced Bairnhouse had told him about Jake's intention to venture into the gangzone of London in search of Dan and of Nancy Sands. Bairnhouse hadn't heard from Jake since then and had no notion where he might be.

Whistling absently, Gomez crossed Piccadilly Circus, turned onto a quirky lane, and entered the Phantom Ship Pub.

The place was dark and dank and smelled of the seashore at low tide. A few bundled-up customers sat, mostly singly, at the rickety tables. The bartender was a huge black man wearing a candy-striped tunic, a sailor cap, and a large glittering golden earring. There was a jeweler's loupe stuck in his left eye, and he was tinkering with something green and feathery that was spread out on the ebony counter in front of him.

"Know anything about electronics, mate?" he inquired as Gomez crossed the dim room.

"Very little."

"It's this arfing parrot, do you see?"

Gomez leaned an elbow on the bar. "What's the trouble?"

"Well now, he's a robot bird."

"I deduced that, soon as I got a glimpse of his circuit board."

"He won't curse."

"What good's a parrot who isn't foul-mouthed?"

"Exactly, mate. You've hit the basic problem square on the noggin, you have." The big bartender poked at the mechanical bird's innards with a tiny silver screwdriver. "I mean to say, he sits on his ruddy perch all day, don't he now, and recites moony love poetry and sentimental drivel. Once in a great while, if I swats him a good one, he'll give out with a halfhearted 'My goodness' or a 'Dear me.' "

"That's not what's required," agreed Gomez sympathetically. "Now then, I'm supposed to meet Mrs. Humphry Ward in your estimable bistro."

"Aye, she's over in a booth. That one yonder there with its curtain discreetly drawn." He pointed with a beefy forefinger that had several tiny green feathers adhering to it. "What about me bird, do you think?"

"Turn him in on a new one," advised Gomez. "Or learn to accept him as he is, but don't tinker."

Mrs. Humphry Ward was an ample woman, blonde at the moment and about forty. She smiled up at Gomez as he entered and raised her mug of foamy beer in salute. "Here's to good times, Sid."

He sat opposite, resting both elbows on the slightly slanting tabletop. "Tell me about Dr. Danenberg."

Mrs. Humphry Ward pointed at the ceiling with a puffy thumb. "The dear lady is going to be traveling to the Caribbean Colony," she said. "That's one of those satellite resorts for the highfaluting and them as pretends they are. She's set to depart at four-twelve this very afternoon. Traveling, she is, under the name of Alice M. Dobson."

"Bueno," he commented. "What goes on up there?"

"The usual foolishness," replied his informant. "They've got hotels, casinos, fake palm trees. Also, so I hear, that balmy Excalibur bunch has its secret headquarters up there somewhere." She held up a forefinger. "That bloke who calls himself King Arthur II, along with his missus, is also a resident of the Colony. But they live openly, nothing clandestine or furtive about them two, in a villa on one of the simulated islands."

"Any Tek activities thereabouts?"

"Well, the British Teklords own a big piece of the place," she replied. "I don't know if they're in cahoots with those Excalibur loons or not."

Gomez nodded slowly. "I've been having trouble tracking down my partner," he told her. "Have you heard anything about him?"

She asked, "Do you know a newsman named Denis Gilford?"

"Nope. What's he have to do with—"

"Gilford's a first-class pain in the bum who works as a reporter for the *London FaxTimes,*" she said. "I hear tell he contacted your pal Jake Cardigan at least twice and made something of a bloody nuisance of himself. And now he's been asking a lot of questions about Jake."

"Sounds like somebody I ought to chat with."

"I'll provide you with a list of the dives and dumps where Gilford hangs out," she offered. "No extra charge, Sid, seeing as how we're such dear pals from way back."

═32═

". . . COMING AROUND," a metallic voice was saying. "Yes, he's definitely coming out of it."

Jake realized that the robot must be talking about him.

He, somewhat reluctantly, opened his eyes.

He saw Gomez looking concernedly down at him.

"Thought you were a robot," Jake muttered, his voice sounding weak and rusty.

"That was the sawbones you heard."

A white-enameled medibot appeared beside Jake's partner. "You're in remarkably good shape for a man your age, sir."

"Thanks." With Gomez's help, Jake sat up. He discovered he was atop Marj's bed. "This is where I made a major mistake."

"Don't tell me you mixed romance with duty?"

"Sort of," he admitted. "How'd you find me?"

"Oh, an *hombre* named Denis Gilford was most helpful in providing me with leads. He mentioned that you'd taken up with Marj Lofton," explained Gomez. "Eventually I got around to looking for you here in her little *hacienda*."

"Gilford was helpful?"

"After I dangled him out a high window by his ankles, *sí*."

Jake asked, "How long have I been out?"

"Ten or twelve hours. I fetched this reliable and discreet medibot to give you a reviving injection soon as I found you down in that impressive hidden lab. Somebody used a stungun on you, *amigo*."

"Yeah, that I remember."

The robot suggested, "You'd better remain in bed for at least a day, sir."

"No, we've got to get up to the Caribbean Colony," said Jake.

Gomez said, "I was coming to tell you the same thing. It seems that Dr. Danenberg, as well as—"

"Dan's up there, that's almost certain."

"Who's got him?"

"I think it's a combination of Excalibur people and Teklords."

"They're making SuperTek up there," said his partner. "I imagine that's why friend Sands was extracted from the hoosegow, to help them manufacture and distribute the stuff."

"What the hell is SuperTek?"

"To put it simply, it's immune to Professor Kittridge's anti-Tek system."

"You mentioned that Dr. Danenberg is—"

"The good doctor is pretty certainly passing along recipes concocted by the old prof himself," said Gomez. "This Caribbean Colony sounds like it's a hotbed of SuperTek activity."

"Yeah, and the Excalibur folks must be helping to fund the Teklab. They'll use their share of the profits to topple the democracy here in England and dump that nitwit Arthur on the throne."

"Wouldn't be the first revolution funded by drug money. Soon as you're feeling chipper enough, we—"

"We've got to get up there right now." With some assistance from his partner, he left the bed and tried standing. He fought against the nausea and dizziness he felt and, slowly, it faded away. "It was Marj who used the stungun on me. I haven't told you why."

"A lovers' spat maybe?"

"C'mon, Sid. She wanted to keep me on the sidelines for a while."

"What exactly is her part in this mess?"

"She used to be an expert in robotics," he said. "Since settling in England she built an android replica of her brother."

"Wasn't her real brother enough for her?"

"He's dead."

"She sounds a trifle morbid."

"Her brother fought in the last Brazil War,

got hooked on Tek, and ended up working for Bennett Sands in one of his undercover Tek operations down there," said Jake. "Marj believes Sands had her brother killed."

"Momentito," requested Gomez. "You're not about to tell me that her late sibling was a lean lad with a bushy moustache and an earring made out of a chunk of Brazilian coinage?"

"Her brother Richard—that is, the android dupe she built—is the Unknown Soldier."

"Madre."

"And by now she's sent him up to the Caribbean Colony to find Sands and kill him."

"Sands nobody'll miss. But if Dan and Nancy are nearby, they could get hurt in the spillover."

"Yeah, and Marj is hours ahead of us," he said. "We have to rush up there."

The medibot shook his head. "That isn't wise."

"A hell of a lot of what I do isn't," said Jake.

"Sure, it fits," said Gomez confidently. Holding both arms out at his sides, he did a slow turn on their stateroom floor. "A bit snug, admittedly, across the middle."

"Definitely snug," agreed Jake. Like his partner, he was wearing a dark blue blazer with the familiar Newz logo emblazoned on the breast pocket in crimson.

"Natalie was in a hurry and had to guess at the sizes."

"You sure you want to collaborate with her from here on?"

"That's why I contacted her, *amigo*," answered Gomez. "It seems to me this is a feasible way for you and I to slip unobtrusively into the Caribbean Colony." He tugged at the bottom of his coat. "Nat's arranged to interview the would-be King Arthur II for Newz. We tag along, posing as her colleagues, until we're safely aboard the satellite."

"It may work." Jake crossed to the window. They were aboard the *Bahama Queen,* a luxury shuttle that traveled between London and the Caribbean Colony.

Gomez burnished the Newz crest on his pocket with his knuckles. "Once there, Nat'll pretend to do the interview while we sneak off to track Bennett Sands to his lair."

"Keep in mind," said Jake, turning away from the view of silent space, "that the Unknown Soldier is also hunting for him."

"We're smarter than an andy," his partner pointed out. "Therefore, even though he's got a head start, we can beat him to the goal."

"This Richard Lofton simulacrum has found and killed several others," reminded Jake. "And he's got Marj coaching him."

Gomez took another critical look at himself in the wall mirror. "Too bad these blazers only come in this drab color," he observed. "Well, let's join Nat up on Deck 7."

Their cabin was on Level 5 and they rode a circular ramp to Level 7.

"Natalie and that snide robot cameraman of hers should be awaiting us in Bob the Beachcomber's Cafe." Gomez tugged again at his blazer in hope of getting it to fit somewhat better.

The corridor they were walking along was lined with a mixture of shops, offices, restaurants, and saloons.

As they approached the Calypso Bar & Grill, the rattan doors swung open. A large, thickset man in a bright plaid suit emerged.

Casually, Gomez nudged his partner. "Strive to look like a newsman," he advised out of the corner of his mouth.

The big man glanced at Gomez, took two steps, did a take, and started reaching inside his plaid coat. "Holy Hannah, it's the Mex!"

"Trouble," said Gomez, "in the form of a Parisian goon."

The partners moved apart.

The goon was tugging out his needlegun.

Jake sprinted forward, then dove right at him.

He butted the gunman hard in the stomach, sending him tottering backwards.

"Son of a gun," observed the big man as he suddenly sat down on his tailbone.

"Another one," warned Gomez, turning toward the second big man who was coming out of the bar.

Jake meantime chopped the needlegun out of the man's grasp. He rose deftly to his feet and then tugged the man upright by the lapels of his plaid coat.

Jake hit him twice on the chin.

The man sighed and fell down again.

Gomez had used his stungun on the second assailant. Eyeing the rattan doors, he said, "That must be the entire set of heavies, *amigo*."

Nobody else came out of the Calypso Bar & Grill.

Jake suggested, "Let's drag these louts to a quiet spot and have a talk. This one ought to come to in a few minutes."

"I noticed a laundry room back around the bend." Gomez bent, grabbed the wrists of the stunned hood, and began dragging him down the corridor. "That ought to do."

— 33 —

As soon as they'd all checked into the Nassau
Palace Hotel, they gathered in Jake's room.

"Basically my stratagem worked." Gomez
was standing with his back to the wide window
that gave a sweeping view of palm trees, red-
tiled rooftops, and golden beaches. "Jake and
I were able to smuggle ourselves here safely by
pretending to be journalists."

"From what you told me about those hoodlums who jumped you," put in Natalie from the
wicker sofa, "your disguise as Newz staffers
didn't fool anyone."

"Those goons just happened to be journey-
ing up here on the same shuttle," Gomez
pointed out. "We met purely by chance."

"I mentioned at the time that you first suggested this scheme that you weren't alert
enough looking, Gomez, to pass as a reporter."

"What say we can this spatting?" suggested

Sidebar, who was stationed near the door with metallic arms folded. "We're supposed to be here to plot strategy."

Jake, from his chair near the viewindow, said, "The lout that we persuaded to confide in us was en route here to report to a fellow named Elisha Clover."

"Clover manages a hostelry called the Tropics Inn," added Gomez.

"He seems to be tied in with the Teklords," said Jake. "I'll check up on him first."

Gomez said, "I've already arranged for some local informants to have Dr. Danenberg's gadding about monitored. Soon as she lights in an interesting spot, I'll go take a look."

"And you'll go ahead with the King Arthur II interview," Jake said to Natalie.

"It seems to me, and keep in mind that I've been expertly ferreting out important secrets for a good long while now, that I'd be of more use tagging along with Gomez."

"*Chiquita,* this is a team," reminded Gomez. "Your chore during this important initial phase of our joint operation is to create a small diversion."

The robot inquired, "When did I volunteer to be part of this half-baked combo? I'm a star, not a mere—"

"Control your pride," Natalie advised her cameraman. "If I can demean myself, so can you, Sidebar."

Jake stood. "Let's try to meet back here in, say, two hours."

"None of you," mentioned the robot, "may be in any shape for a rendezvous by then."

A simulated breeze was blowing across the bright sunlit patio of the villa. It caught at the genealogical chart that King Arthur II was holding up, rattled the paper for several seconds before lifting the chart completely free of the king's pudgy fingers.

"Jove, that's annoying." Arthur hopped clear of his wicker chair and went dashing across the mosaic tiles to snatch at the fleeing chart. "Gwenny, my dear, mightn't we turn down that beastly wind a bit, do you think?"

"I find the breeze most refreshing," said his wife, a plump blonde woman who was seated on a wicker settee. "As I'm sure Miss Dent does."

"Well, I mean to say, my dear," he said, catching the chart and clutching it to his chest, "a breeze is one thing, but a ruddy typhoon is something else altogether, eh?"

"I imagine," said Gwenny, "that Newz didn't ship one of its leading reporters all the way up here simply to hear you natter on about the weather, Arthur dear."

"Deuced unpleasant having a hurricane blowing across one's patio," murmured the man who claimed to be the rightful ruler of Great Britain. Settling into his chair again, he frowned out at the simulated ocean stretching away beyond his patch of real-sand beach. "I assume, Miss Dent, that you'll be able to edit this inane badinage between my dear spouse and myself out of our delightful little interview, eh?"

"We'll make certain you don't look foolish," the reporter promised, nodding at Sidebar.

The robot was standing amidst a grove of authentic palm trees, his camera aimed at King Arthur II. "That's going to take some doing," he muttered.

Arthur, gripping the genealogical chart tightly, held it up to Natalie. "Now then, let's go over this whole jolly thing once again, shall we? These facts and figures make it perfectly clear that I, and I alone, am the rightful heir to the throne of England, if there still were such a thing, don't you know." He traced a line down the middle of the page with his pudgy forefinger.

Natalie asked him, "How far are you prepared to go to see that the monarchy is restored?"

"I intend to pursue my rightful claim."

"No, what I'm talking about is violence," said the reporter. "Would you condone a revolution?"

"I'd prefer, dear girl, to rule England as the result of a bloodless coup, don't you know."

"But do you approve of bloodshed and revolution?"

"I wonder what's become of our tea," said Gwenny.

"I say, my dear, you ought not, really, to intrude these little domestic inquiries into an interview of this magnitude," complained Arthur.

"You know we always have tea at this time each day, Arthur."

"Well, then, old girl, trot off and see what's delaying Rollo." He made a dismissing gesture. "You'll edit out all that last bit of foolishness, eh?"

"Nobody will ever view it," Sidebar assured him, moving closer to the seated pretender to the throne.

"If you'll forgive me for a moment, dear little Miss Dent, and you, too, Mr. Sidebar," said Gwenny as she left her chair, "I must go see what's detaining our servant."

To King Arthur II Natalie said, "What about the Excalibur Movement?"

"One can't always control one's more fanatical followers, what? Obviously, dear child, I don't believe in any sort of violence," he assured her, tapping his knee with the rolled-up chart. "Should, however, overzealous monarchists succeed in getting rid of the current unworkable democratic system that blights my native land, why, I'd be a ruddy fool not to step forward and assume the crown."

"Are you in contact with people from Excalibur?"

"Absolutely not, my dear. I mean to say, a chap in my position can't fraternize with hot-heads of that ilk," replied the would-be king. "Frightfully harmful to one's reputation and all that."

"And you have no idea what their agenda is?"

"Well, I wouldn't go so far as to say that. They do, after all, send me all sorts of procla-mations and manifestos. I have leafed through some of them and so their general aims and . . ." He paused, looked up, and blinked. "Jove, who's that bloke with you, Gwenny?"

The plump blonde had returned from the villa in the company of a large gunmetal robot clad in a checkered suit. "I think you'll find this most interesting, Miss Dent," she said. "This mechanical chap's just now delivered this most interesting snapshot to me." She moved over to Natalie's chair to hand her a small three-dimensional photo.

Somewhat blurry, it showed Natalie and Gomez walking arm in arm along a wintry Paris thoroughfare. "Oh, yes, this is my fiancé and I," she said, dropping the picture to her lap. "He doesn't, I'm the first to admit, take a very flattering photograph. Actually, as Side-bar will testify, he—"

"Nonsense, my dear," cut in Gwenny. "That odious little Latin you were recently hobnob-bing with in France is a well-known shamus. An operative for the Cosmos Detective

Agency—and someone who's intent on causing us no end of trouble and grief."

Natalie nodded at her robot cameraman, but before Sidebar could produce a weapon the robot in the check suit fired a disabler at him.

Sidebar stiffened, then dropped to the patio stones and hit with a resounding bong.

Arthur jumped up, scowling from the fallen cameraman to his wife. "I say, old girl, what the deuce is the meaning of all this?" he asked, perplexed. "It rather, I mean to say, plays the devil with my interview, now doesn't it?"

"Oh, Arthur dear, do be still." Gwenny took a stungun out of her pocket, aimed it at Natalie, and fired.

═34═

OCEAN SPRAY HIT Gomez in the face as his watertaxi zoomed over the glittering blue sea toward Lazarus Cay. It was, all in all, a very believable illusion.

As the taxi docked, its voxbox said, "Have a nice day."

"I intend to." Gomez, still wearing the Newz blazer, climbed up the yellow neowood steps to the impressive white beach.

On a pedestal a few yards off stood a larger-than-life android replica of the entrepreneur Sunny Lazarus. "Hi there, fella," called the android. "Welcome to my island. I'm Sunny Lazarus."

"I didn't realize you were this tall," commented Gomez as he approached the figure on the pedestal.

"What sort of fun did you have in mind?" The android was nearly eight feet tall and had blond wavy hair, a deep tan, and a spotless white suit. "Would you like to try an exciting and scrupulously honest game of chance in my entirely refurbished posh casino? Or, if gaming isn't your cup of tea, there's the gala Lazarus Follies in the grand—"

"Actually, I'm on a more serious mission. Which way is the cemetery?"

"Hey, you're absolutely right. It isn't all fun on Lazarus Cay. No indeed," said the android. "I also offer the best-equipped crematorium in the universe and one of the loveliest cemeteries. Are you, I imagine, paying a visit to a loved one?"

"I'm just anxious to browse around. I'm getting along in years and I decided it's time to start contemplating my own final—"

"A wise move, fella, a very wise move. And I can promise you we'll come up with a purchase plan that's just right for your pocketbook." The big android pointed to his right. "What you want is Pathway 3. Should you have any questions along the route, why, there are plenty Sunny Lazaruses around to help you out. I may be a very important and wealthy man, yet I'm never too busy to lend a hand."

"Much obliged." Gomez took the indicated path, which wound through a dense simulated jungle.

Midway along the wide pathway he encountered another Sunny Lazarus on a pedestal.

"Hi there, fella. Feeling gloomy, I'll bet."

"I am, *sí*. Talking to too many andies in a row always does that to me."

"Hey, no, fella, you're missing my point. I was being sympathetic because you're obviously on the way to our impressive, well-maintained cemetery. Not a happy occasion, and thus—"

"Truth to tell, I'm visiting the crypt of an uncle who died and left me several million dollars. I'm happy as a clam." Smiling, he continued on his way.

The cemetery stood in a well-groomed three-acre clearing. Pausing at the high, wrought-iron gateway, Gomez scanned the place. Then, nodding, he started along a graveled path that led to a sparkling fountain.

Hunched up on a white bench amidst the gravemarkers sat a small, frail man bundled up in a heavy plaid thermocoat. "You took your sweet time getting here, Gomez."

"I rushed here soon as I got your message, Chill." He sat next to the informant.

Frowning at the plashing fountain, Chill Kaminsky said, "I been freezing my ass off out here."

"I had a similar experience in Paris recently," confided Gomez. "Although, if you don't mind my saying so, the Caribbean Colony strikes me as being a bit on the warmish side."

"You know I got a tricky metabolism."

"*Sí*. Now, where's Dr. Danenberg?"

"That's the problem, isn't it? That's why I buzzed you, Gomez," he explained. "I tailed the lady to that big floral shop over there by that row of tombs. She went in about two hours back but she never came out."

"And she isn't still within?"

"Naw. I went in finally to price some gladiolas," said Chill. "Not a trace of her, and I nosed around thoroughly."

"I'd best wander in and see what I can learn."

"Pay me first so I can get home and warm up."

Gomez passed him two $100 Banx notes. *"Gracias,* Chill."

The informant got up, buttoned the thermocoat up to his chin, and went shuffling away across the green fields of the Lazarus Cay Cemetery.

Rising, Gomez brushed at the Newz crest on his breast pocket. He went strolling along a path that led to the domed flower shop.

He pushed through the opaque plastiglass door and was surrounded by the powerful scent of hundreds of unseen flowers. "Howdy, I'm a roving reporter with Newz and I think there might be a dandy human interest story in . . . But perhaps not."

He'd noticed that the burly clerk behind the counter had drawn a lazgun.

* * *

He didn't feel as good as he usually did.

Usually, whenever he was alive again, the Richard Lofton android felt just fine. He'd concentrate on breathing in and out and everything was great. It was almost as though he'd never died at all.

Down here now, deep in the bowels of the Caribbean Colony, he didn't feel all that happy. Sure, he'd been doing his job very well. The stupid wig Marj had made him wear and the expensive tourist suit had fooled everybody.

No one had looked at him funny. He'd checked into a nice hotel and then set about his business.

So far he'd only had to use his stungun on one person. That was the stupid woman who managed this Central Computer Room way down here. He hadn't been able to con her the way he had the others.

But he'd fiddled with the secsystem in a way his sister had taught him, so nobody would suspect anything was wrong for several hours.

What he was unhappy about was that his sister had had to fool around with Jake Cardigan.

He wasn't exactly jealous, but he just didn't like the idea.

Shaking his head, he walked along a metallic corridor and into the small room that housed the main computer for the entire colony.

"She didn't have to hop in bed with the guy," Richard said to himself as he glanced around the cold, gray-walled room. "We're smart, Sis and I. We always find them."

He seated himself at a screen, massaging his knuckles while he studied the keyboard.

If you asked the computer the right questions in the right way, you could find out anything.

And Marj had drilled him, over and over, on just exactly how to ask the questions.

He sat there, smiling faintly, breathing evenly in and out.

This computer was going to tell him, sooner or later, just where Bennett Sands was hiding here on the satellite.

That made Richard feel a little better, but not as good as he ought to feel.

—=35=—

THE FIRST PIRATE wore a dirty eyepatch over his left eye socket and a tattered headrag. With a wicked knife gripped in his jagged, stained teeth, he came clumping across the floor of the chill, stone-walled room in pursuit of the pale blonde young woman in the frilly eighteenth-century frock.

She stumbled, crying out, and fell to the gray stones.

Two more pirates dashed into the room, each waving a cutlass. One of them had a thick, tangled red beard.

The girl screamed as the eyepatched buccaneer touched the tip of his knife to her throat.

The plump woman standing next to Jake on the balcony overlooking the scene remarked, "Well, I think it serves her right. She's been flirting shamelessly with him."

Nodding, Jake moved toward the edge of the

group of seven tourists who were taking this Pirate Castle Tour with him.

"Those of you who don't want to watch the grisly climax of this authentic holographic recreation of life in piratical times," announced Elisha Clover from the edge of the group, "can go down into the dungeon, using Staircase 5 on your left. The torture sequence will be recreated there in exactly seven minutes."

Clover was a small man of forty, his hair a pale shade of blond. On the left lapel of his sky-blue suit was a litebadge that flashed— TROPICS INN TOURS.

While two of the tourists headed toward Staircase 5, Jake eased up close to the hotel manager. "It's simply wonderful the way you conduct these tours yourself, Mr. Clover," he said. "When I heard that, why, I was truly impressed and I knew I had to sign up."

"The personal touch is what's so darned important in this, or any business." Clover was watching the trio of rough pirates start to tear the authentic clothes off the helpless young woman below. "There are, as you no doubt are aware, several excellent hotels up here in the Colony, yet our Tropics . . . awk!"

"That's a stungun poking in your side," explained Jake quietly. "Just start up Staircase 3 if you will."

"But I'm obliged to conduct these people to—"

"Folks . . ." Jake, his body masking the gun,

turned toward the group. "A small emergency has come up, meaning that Mr. Clover and I will have to leave you for just a very few minutes," he told them, grinning. "We'll all meet again down in the dungeon."

Two more prods with the gun barrel persuaded the hotel man to commence climbing.

When they were in a small, shadowy room off the stairway, Jake asked Clover, "Where have they got Dan Cardigan?"

The blond man shuffled backwards until he bumped into a carved pirate chest. "Really, sir, I'm afraid I have no idea what—"

"He's my son."

"You're Jake Cardigan. Damn, I should have—"

"Where?"

"You don't seem to understand, Cardigan." Clover sank down and sat on the chest. "I couldn't possibly betray the people I—"

"What happens if you do?"

"I'll be reprimanded. Probably they'll have me worked over, and I really can't tolerate physical pain or—"

"How do you feel about death?"

"Eh? How's that?"

"If you don't tell me where my son is," said Jake evenly, "I'll kill you. Here and now."

The hotel manager blinked, swallowed. "You can't kill anyone with a stungun."

Tucking the gun into its holster, Jake moved ahead. "With my bare hands, Clover."

He swallowed again, glancing up at the stone ceiling. "Very well," he said after a moment. "I'll tell you how to get to them—your son and the girl."

"Thanks," said Jake.

The flower shop clerk had crinkly orangish hair, and a multitude of freckles dotted his broad flat face. His suit was of a brilliantly colored floral pattern, and the lazgun he held pointed at an important portion of Gomez had an intricately filigreed barrel. "Hoist the mitts, palsy walsy," he suggested.

"I can understand why you might not care to be interviewed by Newz." The detective smiled and started walking up to the plastiglass counter. "But there's certainly no need to pull—"

"Stop right there," ordered the clerk. "And—no kidding—get those paws in the air."

Gomez halted near a man-size plaz statue of an angel. There were three others around the place. "Okay, we can scratch the interview," he offered amiably. "I'll just buy a bunch of posies and be on my—"

"Dr. Danenberg warned us about you, Gomez."

"Warned? Nay, surely she meant to tell you that I ought to be allowed free . . . Excuse me." He paused, then sneezed violently. "Allowed free access to all the facilities hereabouts and . . . excuse me." He sneezed again.

"What the hell's wrong with you anyhow, buddy?"

Eyes squinting, shoulders hunching, Gomez nodded at his surroundings. "Didn't Dr. Danenberg mention that . . . Oops!" He sneezed twice, swaying, tottering nearer the angel. "Mention that I'm allergic . . . Oh, boy!" He sneezed three times and ended up standing just to the right of the large statue. "Allergic to flowers."

"We don't have any real flowers here, jerk," the clerk informed him as he moved his gun to keep it trained on him. "Our stock is all plaz and holographic."

Gomez pointed upward with one of his raised hands. "It's all those . . . oops!" He sneezed twice, then twice more. He put an arm around the angel's waist to steady himself. "All those floral perfumes you're piping in here."

"Yeah? They are kind of sickly sweet now you mention it . . . but I never saw anybody have a fit before."

"Allergies are . . ." Gomez sneezed vigorously three more times. He clutched the statue with both arms.

All at once the angel was falling forward, heading right for the counter and the clerk.

"You dimwit!" The freckled man took a protective jump back out of range as the heavy statue came slamming down onto the countertop.

Gomez was in motion, too.

He ran, leaped clean over the shattering counter, and landed on the clerk before the orange-haired man could get his gun aimed again.

Gomez took hold of the man's gun hand by the wrist and smacked it back against the wall. The freckled fingers let go of the filigreed weapon.

Two sharp jabs to the chin dropped the clerk to the flower shop floor.

Stepping over him, Gomez very carefully opened the door to the back room. He had his stungun in his hand when he crossed the threshold.

There was no one there.

The room contained several tables covered with vases holding imitation blossoms.

There was another doorway at the far side of the room. It led to a ramp that slanted down to a belowground tunnel.

Gomez started along the ramp.

—=36=—

DAN WAS SEATED at a small portatable near the suite window, absently staring out at the simulated sea. A tray of food rested on the table. "It doesn't make any sense," he was saying.

Nancy was seated at a similar table nearby, ignoring her meal. "No, everything makes sense," she said, "eventually. Sometimes, though, you have to think about it for a while."

"I don't know—for a long time now I've had the feeling that there was something that my father wasn't telling me," he said. "Maybe he's known that my mother, if what you say is true . . ." He trailed off, pushing back his chair and standing.

"I'm afraid it is true, everything I told you, Dan."

"But that means she's been lying to me." He stood close to the window, forehead almost touching it. "Lying about why we came to England, about what she's doing . . . Shit, about everything."

"Most parents lie. Ours, it turns out, happen to be especially good at it."

The door to the suite whispered open. Jake came in, dragging a stungunned guard. "Dan, are you okay?"

Dan remained where he was, mouth open. "Dad, how'd you get here?"

"I used my wits . . . and when that didn't work, I used a stungun."

"I was hoping you'd find us."

"We have to get out of here quickly," said Jake as the door closed behind him. He propped the unconscious man against the wall. "I've been damn lucky so far, but we better move now. Detailed explanations can come later."

"I figured you'd come looking for me." Running across the room, he hugged his father.

Jake hugged back. "Okay, let's go."

"Nancy has to come, too." His son stepped back. "She isn't—"

"I can't stay here, Mr. Cardigan." She had left the table. "You have no reason to trust me, I know, but—"

"We'll thrash that out later," he told her. "Right now we have to leave."

The door slid open again. Kate Cardigan came into the room. Her face was pale, frowning. "None of you is going to leave," she told them. In her right hand she held a lazgun.

Natalie awakened.

Directly in front of her, taking up nearly one entire wall of the large room she found herself in, was a vast animated painting of the original King Arthur. The handsome, bearded monarch was seated at his Round Table with a sampling of his knights.

The reporter was seated in a metal chair and her right arm hurt. Standing beside her, she noticed now, was Hilda Danenberg.

The doctor was holding a hypogun. "Don't try to stand for a few minutes," she advised. "I just gave you an injection to revive you. That silly woman had her stungun set far too high. You'd have been unconscious for a good day at least."

"How long," asked Natalie, her voice slurred and not quite her own, "have I been out?"

"Oh, not very long."

Across the room Natalie spotted Sidebar. He was lying immobile, flat on his back and not functioning. "Why'd you revive me so soon?"

"I wished to talk to you," explained the doctor. "And so does Mr. Pettiford."

"Well, yes, I surely do." A tall, lanky man had been standing behind Natalie's chair. He came around into view, smiling thinly. "We want to know, for instance, how many spies and saboteurs you brought up here with you."

"I don't, unlike your crony here, hang around with spies and such," Natalie assured him. "I happen to be an accredited reporter for Newz, and as I'm sure you must be fully aware, you people have seriously violated my rights as—"

"What about Jake Cardigan?" asked Dr. Danenberg.

"Last I heard, he was in London," the reporter answered. "I do now and then, not by choice I can assure you, bump into his boorish partner, a fellow named Gomez, but truly, I have no official connection with the Cosmos Detective Agency whatsoever."

Pettiford inquired, "Didn't this Gomez come along with you to the Caribbean Colony?"

"I'm afraid I'm not exactly clear as to who you are." Natalie frowned. "Which of the lunatic groups do you—"

"Well, yes, I can fill you in. I'm a Senior Knight First Class in the Excalibur Movement," answered the lanky man. "That means I'm one of the heads of the whole—"

"That's fine. Maybe I can interview you sometime." Natalie attempted to stand. "As you ought to know, my sole and only reason for coming up to this tacky paradise was in order to prepare an interview with the self-proclaimed King Arthur II." She was managing to stay on her feet. "Since you Excalibur people presumably support him and his claims, I would have thought you'd be grateful for any publicity I provide him. Instead, you seem intent on keeping me a virtual prisoner and—"

"We've had more than enough of your inane babbling." Angry, Dr. Danenberg reached out and slapped her.

Natalie cried out and took a few steps away from her chair. "Smacking a newsperson is not a—"

"Who came here with you?"

"I came alone." Natalie, legs shaky, crossed to where her disabled robot lay. "Of course I was accompanied by Sidebar. But since he's a robot and not a person, I don't imagine you want to count him. So . . ." She brought up a hand to her forehead, swaying. "Darn, I'm a lot dizzier than I thought." Dropping to her knees, she slumped across the robot.

Slipping one hand unobtrusively across the robot's chest, Natalie tapped the button that opened the compartment concealed in his side. There was a compact stungun stowed there.

"We already frisked your cameraman," said Dr. Danenberg, impatience sounding in her voice. "We have the stungun, dear."

"That's okay, *amigos*," announced Gomez as he came in by way of a side door. "I have one of my own."

═37═

DAN DIDN'T CRY.

But as he stood there, lips pressed tight together and fists clenched, he was very close to tears.

His mother came farther into the suite. She held the lazgun firmly. "Don't try anything, Jake," warned Kate. "Please—I don't want to have to . . . to kill you."

Jake remained where he was. "So you are involved in all this mess, huh?"

"Sure," she admitted. "Isn't that what you've always suspected?"

"Yeah, but I guess I've been hoping—"

"It's too late for hoping," his ex-wife told him. "You've screwed everything up."

"Kate, you were the one who contacted me," he reminded. "Pleaded with me to find Dan."

"I know, yes, but I . . . I didn't think Danny would end up here," she said. "Or that you'd be able to trace him all this way."

"You should've realized that, since Dan and Nancy were brought here on orders from Sands' partners."

"Yes, I'm aware of that now, but it's too late."

"Mom," said Dan, struggling to control his voice, "I didn't want to believe it when Nancy told me that you were working with her father. But . . . but it's true, isn't it?"

"Yes, Danny. It's true," answered his mother. "But you have to understand why I—"

"They killed people," he said. "They murdered Tek Kids and . . . and I don't know who the hell else. And you . . . you're part of the whole damn thing."

"You simply don't comprehend what's going on," insisted Kate. "This is a multimillion-dollar venture."

"I comprehend that you're collaborating with killers and Tekrunners," said her son. "I comprehend that you screwed up my life and that you've told me lies for . . . shit, for years."

"But, Danny—our share of this will give us financial security for the rest of our lives."

"Dad *was* innocent," said Dan, pointing at Jake. "Completely, wasn't he? It was you and that bastard Bennett Sands who set him up, framed him. You got him sentenced to the goddamn Freezer—and all along you *knew* that he was—"

"Nancy, don't let him talk about your father

that way," cautioned Kate, deep frowns touching her pale forehead.

"My father is a rotten bastard," said Sands' daughter. "When I found that out, I ran away. Unfortunately, that just caused more trouble for Dan."

"Please, both of you—you have to stop talking to me like this," pleaded Kate. "You must see that I'm trying to help you."

"Oh . . . and Dad, too?" asked Dan.

Jake's former wife slowly shook her head. "There's nothing I can do for him," she said. "But, trust me, no harm will come to you or Nancy. You were brought here so that you couldn't tell anyone about what's going on."

"You're standing there telling me that your damned lover is going to kill my father!" shouted Dan. "And you expect me to be grateful to you?"

"Danny, don't yell at me," said his mother. "You don't understand . . . you don't want to understand . . . that whatever I've done, it was for you as well as for myself."

"That's great, Mom. I hadn't thought of it like that, no," said her son. "Every time you jumped in the sack with Bennett, why, it was really to help me."

"You have no right to—"

"Yes, I do. The things you've done give me the right."

"Danny, don't keep on like this."

Dan started walking toward her. "I'll tell

you something else," he said. "I'm going to take that lazgun away from you."

"Danny, don't try it!"

"And the only way you can stop me," he told her, "is by shooting me down."

Gomez, stungun in hand, came strolling into the room where they were holding Natalie. "Are you in passable shape, *chiquita?*" he asked her.

The reporter was still kneeling beside the disabled Sidebar. "I'm not in the best shape I've ever been in, but I'm functioning." Carefully, she started to rise.

Gomez allowed himself to be briefly distracted by her wobbly efforts.

Noticing that, the lanky Pettiford lunged, grabbed up the metal chair the young woman had been sitting in, and hurled it straight at Gomez.

Most of the chair legs caught Gomez in the chest. He fell backwards, sitting hard. His gun hit the floor and spun away.

Dr. Danenberg made a dive for the skittering weapon.

Natalie, on her feet again, ran. She jumped, landing on the stooping doctor's broad back.

While the two women were struggling for possession of the fallen stungun, Gomez devoted his attention to the Excalibur leader.

Pettiford had followed the chair and was

grappling with Gomez, attempting to twist the detective's arm up behind his back.

Jerking free, Gomez rolled and then kicked up.

His boot toe connected with the diving Pettiford's chin.

"Unk," he said, dropping flat.

Gomez got to his knees, grabbed the man up, and delivered three short jabs to his jaw.

Pettiford sagged. Gomez let him sink to the floor and into unconsciousness.

"Bueno," he commented, standing up and looking around.

Natalie, brushing back her hair, was straddling the fallen Dr. Danenberg. The stungun was firmly gripped in her right hand. "Don't think I don't appreciate your daring attempt at a rescue, Gomez," she said, a bit breathlessly. "However, should we ever find ourselves in a similar situation at some future date, I do hope you won't be quite so clumsy."

Bowing, Gomez smiled at her. "Your gracious thanks are most gratefully accepted, *linda,*" he said. "And now I suggest that we have a little chat with the good doctor."

Kate kept the lazgun aimed at her son. "Danny," she said, "don't do this."

He was only a few feet from her now. "Give me the gun," he said and held out his hand.

"I can't."

"Well, you're not going to use it to kill my father. So either shoot me or—"

"Please, Danny, try to understand why I—"

"I understand." He reached out, closing his fingers over the barrel of the lazgun.

Kate, starting to cry, let go of the weapon. She turned, angry, toward Jake. "He's . . . he's just like you."

Dan slipped the gun into his pocket. "Nancy, Dad, we can go now," he said.

They moved single file along the hotel corridor. Dan was in the lead, followed by Nancy and then his mother. Jake brought up the rear.

"You're not going to make it out of here," warned Kate.

"Once we get to the service passages we'll be okay."

"Bennett's in this hotel," his former wife said. "He's at a meeting. As soon as that ends, he's planning to meet me at the kids' room. When he finds them gone, he'll mount a search of the entire satellite."

"Dan, we want that blue door on the right."

"Okay, Dad." Slowing, Dan approached the door. He opened it, slowly and carefully, and entered the blank-walled corridor beyond.

Kate said, "Bennett will kill you."

"He's tried before." Jake urged her into the passageway.

"If you simply give up, turn the kids over to him, then you have a chance."

"We'll travel in silence from here on."

"I'm trying to help you, Jake, to save your damn life."

"It's funny, Kate. Somehow I find it tough to trust you."

Near the end of this section of corridor was another blue door.

"Do we want this doorway, Dad?"

"Yeah, and then take the down ramp on the left."

Before any of them reached the door, it came snapping open.

Bennett Sands, a lazgun in his hand, stepped into the hallway. "Well, Jake Cardigan," he said, smiling. "Just the man I was hoping to meet."

=38=

THE LEFT SLEEVE of Sands' jacket hung empty. He was a pale man, puffy-faced, and he continued to smile in a smug, self-satisfied way. "As I recall, Cardigan, you invaded my privacy once before."

"Down in Mexico, yeah."

"Thanks to you, and your IDCA friends, I lost an arm."

"Hello, Father." Nancy took a few steps away from Dan.

Not looking directly at his daughter, keeping his attention centered on Jake, Sands said, "I'll be talking to you later, young lady. You've caused me one hell of a lot of trouble."

"It's mutual," she said.

"We'll discuss all this later, Nan."

"After you murder Jake Cardigan, do you mean?"

"That'll be quite enough," he told her.

"Now, Cardigan, I want you to walk over here to me."

"Danny, don't!" Kate suddenly cried out. She rushed at her son, throwing both arms tight around him. "Bennett—he's got my gun."

"Danny, I'm surprised at you." Sands moved his lazgun so that it pointed at the boy. "Why, I've been a second father to you."

"I still have my first father." Dan let go of the lazgun he'd been trying to slip free of his jacket pocket. "I don't need you, Bennett."

"Wait—don't try it, Cardigan." Sands returned his attention to Jake.

Jake had been reaching for the stungun inside his coat. "You're not too popular with the younger generation," he remarked, putting both his hands, palms out, in front of him.

"When I get time, I'll brood about that."

Kate retrieved her weapon from her son's pocket. "Don't, please, try anything like that again, Danny."

Jake asked, "You're going to be running the SuperTek operation, are you, Sands?"

"I'm going to be one of several equal partners, rather."

Nodding, Jake said, "And is Professor Kittridge one of the other partners?"

"Oh, yes," replied Sands. "Yes, Cardigan, your current mistress's father is in with us."

"And you're also active in this Excalibur Movement, huh?"

Laughing, Sands said, "Lunatic funds are as

good as any," he said. "They've financed a substantial part of things thus far."

"Including your escape." Nancy moved over beside Dan.

"Please don't interrupt the conversation, young lady," cautioned her father. "But, actually, now I think of it, the conversation's over. Cardigan—very carefully hand over the weapons that you're carrying."

"He's got a stungun," Kate informed him. "I don't know what else."

Sands said, "All right, Cardigan. Let's have the stungun—" He stopped speaking and his eyes went wide.

A red door across the corridor had suddenly opened. Richard Lofton, carrying a stungun and a lazgun, stepped through the doorway.

"It's been a long time, hasn't it, Bennett?" he said.

Dr. Danenberg touched her right palm to the recplate on the office door and it slid open. "In here," she said in a sour, disgruntled voice. She remained standing in the chill corridor.

"You're certainly grouchy," observed Gomez, urging her into the room ahead of him and carefully scanning its interior as they crossed the threshold.

Three of the walls were of gray metal and the fourth was of one-way seethrough plastiglass. Out beyond that stretched a large lab, where roughly two dozen robots, a dozen androids, and seven or eight humans were all at work at long white tables.

"Bueno," commented Gomez as the door whooshed shut behind them. "We've finally found the Teklab that we've been seeking, *chiquita."*

Natalie walked up close to the seethrough wall. "I wish these dreadful nitwits hadn't incapacitated Sidebar," she said ruefully. "Some footage on this clandestine Tek chip factory, coupled with my usual insightful description of things, would make a darn nifty news segment."

"Sit down in that chair yonder, doc," suggested Gomez, gesturing with his stungun. "Fold your hands sedately in your lap, *por favor."*

"I'm truly sorry it was your leg and not your neck that you broke."

"Let's see if we can't maintain the chummy relationship we've had thus far." He rested his backside against the edge of the rubberoid desk. "I take it that you and Prof Kittridge didn't really split up?"

"You can assume any damn thing you wish, Mr. Sanchez."

"Gomez," he corrected, smiling. "I already know that you've been popping up to NorCal and sneaking visits with him. I figure somehow he managed to slip you some handy tips on how to manufacture SuperTek." He pointed at the busy lab with a thumb.

Folding her arms, the doctor said nothing.

Natalie said, "Your interviewing technique, if you don't mind my saying so, isn't as smooth and efficient as it might be."

"I know, *sí*," he admitted. "Sometimes, in my overzealous quest for information, I start slapping people around. It's a definite character flaw, but there you are." He smiled more broadly at Dr. Danenberg. "Now then—about Kittridge?"

"Yes, he is involved," she answered in a low, tight-lipped way. "The idea for SuperTek is his. He and Sands were already planning this even before all that mess down in Mexico."

"Muy triste." Gomez shook his head slowly. "It's sad to think that a man of his capabilities could be tempted by vast sums of loot to sell out his species."

"Are we going to loiter hereabouts all the livelong day while you pontificate in Spanish?" Natalie turned away from the see-through wall.

"Patience, *chiquita*. A little moralizing now and then is good for the old *alma*." Gomez eased over to the vidphone alcove. "I note they have a bugproof phone here. I'll put through a satcall to the London office of the International Drug Control Agency and report our findings. They, in turn, will dispatch a paddy wagon up here to this den of thieves."

"But can we trust the IDCA?"

Gomez replied, "I know an *hombre* in the

London branch who's true blue." He sat down facing the phonescreen. "Soon as I finish, we'll go rendezvous with Jake."

"How do we determine just exactly where he is at the moment?"

"Dr. Danenberg is going to tell us," he explained. "Or rather, she'll inform us where Dan and Nancy are being kept. Jake should be somewhere in the vicinity."

☰39☰

RICHARD LOFTON SMILED as he moved, slowly, closer to Sands. "I haven't changed much over the years, have I, Bennett?" He held both guns aimed at him.

"No, not much at all, Dick." Sands' lazgun was pointing at the newcomer.

"Don't try anything funny, Cardigan," warned Lofton, glancing quickly at him. "I look just like I did when you ordered me killed, don't I, Bennett?"

Sands shook his head. "You know I had nothing to do with any attempt on your life."

Lofton laughed. "Sure, you did, Bennett," he said. "Hell, the guys you hired for the job told me all about it, right before they killed me. Did they report back to you? Give you all the details? See, what they did—and it amused the shit out of them when they told me their plans—they cut my body up into pieces. Out in

303

the fucking jungle this was, you know, Bennett, so you can imagine—"

"What the hell are you talking about, Dick? You're still alive and—"

"I've been making quite a name for myself, Bennett," he said. "Lots of people, you included, thought I wouldn't amount to much. But, shit, I'm famous."

"I wasn't aware of that."

"That's because I'm famous under another name," he explained. "I'm the Unknown Soldier."

Sands said, "I don't think I've heard of you."

"Sure, you have. Fact is, some of your buddies have been imitating me. Isn't that so, Cardigan?"

"Yeah. They tried to make Joseph Bouchon's murder look like one of yours," Jake answered. "They wanted to keep him from digging into their SuperTek operations."

"They were assholes," he said. "They didn't come anywhere close to aping my style."

"Richard, what we'll have to do is sit down and talk, get everything settled between us," suggested Sands. "Right now, as you can see, I have to settle with Cardigan."

"Bennett, hey, you've got it all wrong." Lofton walked a few paces closer to him. "I'm here, see, to settle a score with you. You're the one we wanted to kill right at the start, except you were unreachable in that damn maxsec dump in California. So we started with some of the others."

"Listen to reason," said Sands. "I'm holding a lazgun myself. The odds are that—"

"Oh, c'mon, Bennett. I don't give a rat's ass if you kill me again," he told him. "And before you do, I know I can gun you down. Of course, I'd like to be able to slice you up, but I won't insist on—"

"Please," said Kate. "Don't do this. Bennett is perfectly willing to make a generous settlement with you. Aren't you, Bennett?"

"Yes, of course. That would be much better than this foolish standoff, Richard."

Lofton laughed again. "He doesn't get it," he said, shaking his head. "Tell him, Cardigan."

"You really did succeed in killing Richard Lofton years ago in Brazil," Jake explained. "It should be obvious to you by now, Sands, that what you're talking to is a very creditable android."

Sands narrowed his eyes, looking at Lofton. "An android," he said quietly.

"That's right, Bennett," Lofton said. "See, androids don't need money or flattery or any bullshit. I came up here to kill you, you poor son of a bitch."

Kate suddenly lunged at the android, crying out, "No! I won't let you kill him!"

Lofton slapped her aside with the hand holding the stungun.

At the same time Sands aimed and fired his lazgun.

But Lofton fired his lazgun, too.

The beam sliced a deep zigzag line down across the one-armed man's chest.

Sands' shot succeeded in chopping off both the android's legs.

Kate, sobbing, ran to the tottering Sands.

Blood was spurting out of the deep rut in his chest. He dropped to his knees, and drops of blood went splattering all around him on the metallic floor.

Sands tried to speak, but blood came out of his mouth instead of words.

"Bennett, Bennett . . ." Kate put her arms around him, struggling to keep him from falling over.

"Damn," muttered the fallen Lofton. "I still have five more to kill." He ceased to function.

Dan took hold of Nancy's hand. They stood there and watched her father die.

Jake didn't get back to Greater Los Angeles until two days after Xmas.

His first afternoon there he went out to the edge of the Santa Monica Sector. He walked along a stretch of beach, stopping often to stare out at the pale blue ocean.

Gomez caught up with him there toward sundown. "May I trudge along with you, *amigo?*"

Jake shrugged and resumed walking.

His partner said, "I was just over talking to

Bascom at Cosmos. We'll be getting a bonus on the Bouchon case. Plus a handsome share of the eventual reward the IDCA is going to pay us for locating the SuperTek laboratory."

Halting again, Jake looked out toward the horizon. "I'm getting old, Sid," he said finally.

"I've noticed, *sí*. But, being a trusted chum, I haven't mentioned it."

"What I mean is—hell, when we were cops and finished up a case, I usually felt good about it."

"Nobody would expect you to be overjoyed just now. Kate's likely to go to prison; so is Professor Kittridge."

"I probably knew all along that Kate was deeply mixed up in all this," he said, "but I pretended she wasn't."

"Since you were expecting something like this, it probably didn't hit you as hard as it might have."

Jake commenced walking again. "Dan's the one who was hit hard."

"He's tough, though."

"Yeah, but still . . ."

"Hey, he's nearly grown up. You have to quit trying to shelter him from the realities of life."

"I was away too long while he was growing up. Up in the Freezer—maybe even before that—I wasn't around enough."

"Let's switch to the topic of *mañana*," suggested Gomez. "What's he decided to do?"

"Dan's going to stay in England until Nancy Sands is ready to move back to GLA—that shouldn't be too far off," answered Jake. "Then he'll be coming back and living with me."

"*Bueno*. That ought to be good for both of you," he said. "Speaking of Great Britain, there's still no word on the present whereabouts of Marj Lofton. Sundry law enforcers are beating the bushes for her."

"She's probably somewhere building another replica of her brother."

"And how's Beth faring?"

"She's not especially saddened by her father's arrest," answered Jake. "She'll be working up in Berkeley until the anti-Tek system is ready to use."

"At which time you'll get together again?"

"Yeah, probably sometime after the first of the year."

"Well, that's a fairly happy ending to this whole business," his partner observed. "You and Dan together, you and Beth together—oh, and Natalie Dent and a reactivated Sidebar up at the Moonbase Colony covering a story for the next few weeks. Plus which, soon there'll be no more Tek in the world."

Jake said, "Something just as bad is sure to come along."

"But in that short interval between troubles," said Gomez, "we can enjoy ourselves, *amigo*."

STEVEN BRUST

___ *PHOENIX* 0-441-66225-0/$4.50

In the return of Vlad Taltos, sorcerer and assassin, the Demon Goddess comes to his rescue, answering a most heartfelt prayer. How strange she should even give a thought to Vlad, considering he's an *assassin*. But when a patron deity saves your skin, it's always in your best interest to do whatever she wants . . .

___ *JHEREG* 0-441-38554-0/$4.99

There are many ways for a young man with quick wits and a quick sword to advance in the world. Vlad Taltos chose the route of the assassin and the constant companionship of a young jhereg.

___ *YENDI*   0-441-94460-4/$4.99

Vlad Taltos and his jhereg companion learn how the love of a good woman can turn a cold-blooded killer into a <u>real</u> mean S.O.B...

___ *TECKLA* 0-441-79977-9/$4.99

The Teckla were revolting. Vlad Taltos always knew they were lazy, stupid, cowardly peasants...revolting. But now they were revolting against the empire. No joke.

___ *TALTOS* 0-441-18200/$4.99

Journey to the land of the dead. All expenses paid! Not Vlad Taltos' idea of an ideal vacation, but this was work. After all, even an assassin has to earn a living.

___ *COWBOY FENG'S SPACE BAR AND GRILLE*
0-441-11816-X/$3.95

Cowboy Feng's is a great place to visit, but it tends to move around a bit—from Earth to the Moon to Mars to another solar system— and always just one step ahead of whatever mysterious conspiracy is reducing whole worlds to radioactive ash.

For Visa, MasterCard and American Express orders ($15 minimum) call: 1-800-631-8571

FOR MAIL ORDERS: CHECK BOOK(S). FILL OUT COUPON. SEND TO:	**POSTAGE AND HANDLING:** $1.75 for one book, 75¢ for each additional. Do not exceed $5.50.
BERKLEY PUBLISHING GROUP 390 Murray Hill Pkwy., Dept. B East Rutherford, NJ 07073	**BOOK TOTAL** $ _____
NAME_____	**POSTAGE & HANDLING** $ _____
ADDRESS_____	**APPLICABLE SALES TAX** $ _____ (CA, NJ, NY, PA)
CITY_____	**TOTAL AMOUNT DUE** $ _____
STATE_____ZIP_____	**PAYABLE IN US FUNDS.**
PLEASE ALLOW 6 WEEKS FOR DELIVERY. **PRICES ARE SUBJECT TO CHANGE WITHOUT NOTICE.**	(No cash orders accepted.) 315